KEEPING
CHRISTMAS

Books by Dan Walsh

The Unfinished Gift
The Homecoming
The Deepest Waters
Remembering Christmas
The Discovery
The Reunion
What Follows After

THE RESTORATION SERIES with Gary Smalley

The Dance
The Promise
The Desire
The Legacy

KEEPING CHRISTMAS

A Novel

DAN WALSH

Revell

a division of Baker Publishing Group
Grand Rapids, Michigan

© 2015 by Dan Walsh

Published by Revell
a division of Baker Publishing Group
P.O. Box 6287, Grand Rapids, MI 49516-6287
www.revellbooks.com

Printed in the United States of America

Library of Congress Cataloging-in-Publication Data
Walsh, Dan, 1957–
    Keeping Christmas : a novel / Dan Walsh.
        pages ; cm
    ISBN 978-0-8007-2119-0 (pbk.)
    1. Domestic fiction. I. Title.
PS3623.A446K44 2015
813'.6—dc23   2015005640

This book is a work of fiction. Names, characters, places, and incidents are the product of the author's imagination or are used fictitiously.

15   16   17   18   19   20   21   7   6   5   4   3   2   1

1

Judith Winters never understood why they called it Black Friday. Though it might have positive connotations for retail stores, black was also a color associated with mourning and funerals. That was closer to how she felt today. She had been staring at her perfectly brewed cup of coffee long enough for it to go from warm to cold. What time was it now, nine thirty? How'd it get to be nine thirty already?

For her, the day after Thanksgiving had never been about shopping. Even when her two daughters, Anna and Suzanne, had lived at home. Now, *they* had shopped on Black Fridays as soon as they were old enough to drive. Every Thanksgiving evening they rummaged through newspaper flyers looking for the best deals, then got up before the crack of dawn. Judith never tried to stop them. She knew what they'd find out when they were married and had kids of their own. Shopping on

Black Fridays wasn't as much fun with a lot less money in your purse.

They understood that now, her two girls. Even Suzanne, who became a mom this past year. Judith had spoken to both of them at different times yesterday on the phone. Anna in Richmond, Suzanne in Fort Worth. They laughed when Judith asked them how early they'd be hitting the stores today.

But Judith wasn't laughing now. Those conversations were the main reason she'd been sitting here staring at her coffee all this time. They had been talking on the *phone*, not around the dinner table.

Anna was four states away to the north; Suzanne four states to the west. Both spent Thanksgiving Day with their husbands and kids, not here in Mount Dora with her and Stan. Same thing with Brandon, their middle child. Until this year, he and his family had lived in Jacksonville, a two-hour drive from here. They always drove down for Thanksgiving. Not anymore. Now they lived five states away in Denver.

None of her kids had been there. None of her grandkids, either.

This was the first year since Judith and Stan became empty nesters that the nest stayed empty on Thanksgiving. They had roasted a turkey, she and Stan. She'd made her famous homemade mashed potatoes, with a big bowl of piping-hot gravy. String bean casserole, turkey stuffing, cranberry sauce. Pumpkin pie for dessert. All of it on the table. But it wasn't Thanksgiving Day at the Winterses' house. Not with just her and Stan there, and nothing between them but all that food on the table. After Stan said the blessing, they'd hardly talked.

Stan had even left the TV on.

Before he'd left the table, Stan had mentioned one thing.

He saw no reason why they shouldn't keep their usual Black Friday morning tradition alive, even though the kids hadn't come home. "You know what I'm talking about," he'd said. She did. It was the tradition where she would get up and start decorating the house for Christmas and he went bass fishing on Lake Dora with his best friend, Barney.

That was where Stan was right now, with Barney on their little fishing boat. He'd left the house before she'd gotten out of bed. But he'd left her a little present. On the dinette table in front of her sat two boxes marked "Christmas Decorations." He'd brought them in from the garage before he left, the same as he did every year. He'd return before lunch, expecting heated-up turkey leftovers from yesterday and the house all decorated for Christmas, everything except the tree.

He'd bring the Christmas tree in after lunch and set it up in the corner of the living room, expecting her to have it all decorated by dinner. Meanwhile, he and Barney would take a forty-five-minute drive south to Orlando and spend the afternoon stocking up on all the great Black Friday deals at Bass Pro Shop.

This had become the Black Friday tradition for Judith and Stan. Same thing for years. Except for one thing.

Every other year before today, Judith could count on at least one or both of her daughters and her daughter-in-law being there with her all day, and at least some of her grandkids. She'd fill the house with Christmas music and put eggnog and hot chocolate on the table, and they'd spend a pleasant day together, chatting about fond memories and making new ones. Before long, they'd transform the Winters family home into a charming Christmas cottage.

But today, Judith was all alone.

She stood and carried her coffee mug to the sink, poured out the remains, and rinsed it. Staring at the cartons on the table, she realized she had no desire to open them. How could she decorate the house now? Tears welled up in her eyes, and they weren't tied to yesterday's disappointment.

No, these tears belonged to something much worse.

In those same phone conversations with her children yesterday, Judith learned that none of them were coming home for Christmas. The money just wasn't there. She could hardly believe it.

Thanksgiving certainly mattered. But for her, Christmas mattered so much more. She had come to accept the reality that she would no longer get the chance to see her children or grandchildren on a regular basis. But Christmas had been the one occasion she could always count on. It was the one season—and always had been—for making memories. The one time they would always get together and reconnect.

But not this year.

What was the point of decorating the house or even setting up a tree? There'd be no one here to see it, no one to share it with.

2

Are you gonna cast over here?" Barney said. "Because if you are, maybe we should just switch places."

Stan looked at where his lure had just landed, near some maidencane grass just beyond the shoreline. "What are you going on about? Look where that hit. It's still on my half of the boat."

"Maybe. But you hook a good-size bass right there, and he's not gonna know the difference between your side and mine. He'll get all tangled up in my line."

Stan shook his head. Barney could worry about nothing sometimes. "Just sit tight. I'll move it." He reeled in his line and cast it out again toward the back of the boat. "You're just edgy 'cause you got skunked so far, and I picked up two." And they were nice ones, Stan thought. Both over two pounds. Just then, one of the fish made a fuss in the livewell, kicking his tail against the side. "See? He knows I'm talking about him."

"Plenty of time to catch up," Barney said, casting his line out again. "Morning's still young."

Stan glanced at his watch. "Not really. It's almost eleven thirty. Morning's almost over."

"You're kidding, eleven thirty? Time flies when you're having fun."

"That what you're having?" Stan said. "I know I am." Jabbing each other this way was about half of their relationship. Finding ways to one-up each other made up the other half. "There she goes!" Stan got a big bite. He snapped the rod back to set the hook.

"Not again," Barney said.

"Living right, that's all it is." Stan kept the tension tight on the rod, which was bent almost in half, as he reeled the fish in. He steered it toward the back of the boat. "I won't let her tangle you up, if you want to keep casting."

Barney was in between casts. "That's all right. The way that thing's pulling, I think you might need a little help pulling 'er in." He set his rod down and reached for the net.

Stan didn't really want the help, but Barney might be right. "I don't think you need a net here. Just bend a little more at the waist. I'll steer it over to you. There it is. See it?" It was a nice one. Definitely bigger than the other two.

Barney reached into the water and grabbed the splashing fish by the jaw, heaved it up over the side. Stan set his rod to the side and reached for his pliers. "I think it might top four pounds."

"At least," Barney said. He held the catch up so Stan could take the lure out of its mouth. Once free, he held it up higher.

"Now that's a keeper." Stan opened the lid to the livewell, and Barney set the bass inside. Immediately, it began splashing and thumping around. "Letting the other two know who's boss." He closed the lid. "Can't believe you got three, and I still got a big goose egg. Let me see that new lure you're using."

Stan handed the rod over. "It's this new red rattle bait I bought. I saw it on a Bill Dance show. Shake it. You can hear it."

Barney did. "Darn. Sounds just like a baby's rattle."

"He said the bass can hear it too. And they love that bright red color. Flashes in the sun when you reel them back in these shallow waters."

"I'm gonna have to get me one." He stepped back to the front of the boat and rummaged through his tackle box. "In the meantime . . . think I got me a bright red spinnerbait here somewhere. Maybe the bass in this canal have a thing for the color red."

Stan smiled and cast his rattle bait a few feet to the right from his last cast. "Can't beat the weather out here. You see the news this morning? It might snow in Atlanta this afternoon. Here we are in short sleeves." He looked around at the scenery. Today they had trolled down one of the residential canals that came off the Dora canal. All around were nice, newer homes. Not mansions, but definitely bigger than Stan's place and well out of his price range.

"Ever regret how we've ended up?" Barney said.

He must've seen Stan looking at the nice houses. "Not really. I'm not gonna lie, some of these places are nice. But I like our little house. I especially like that it's paid for. I know some guys our age are still working as hard as they did in their twenties, 'cause they got caught in that house trap. They kept buying bigger and better ones, kept restarting those thirty-year mortgages so they could make the higher payments. Now they're stuck." He cast out again. "Nope, that's not for me."

Both Stan and Barney liked to refer to themselves as "semi-retired." Both were a few years away from getting Social Security and Medicare. Both had modest pensions from jobs they'd worked at for decades. Decent income but not enough to live on. So both worked part-time to close the gaps. Stan worked at the Home Depot in Leesburg, a few miles away. Barney at the Lowe's up on 441.

Barney surveyed the scene. "Not for me, either. Besides, they're not happy, those people."

That was what Barney always said about people who lived in fancy homes. He consoled himself about the apparent unfairness in life, saying this was God's way of balancing things out between the haves and the have-nots. The rich got to have nice homes but no happiness with it. Behind those fancy doors, they were fighting all the time, cheating on each other, bored out of their minds.

Stan sometimes would point out that you could use most of those same words to describe a lot of have-nots he knew. He didn't bring it up this time. "I'm thinking we should start heading back pretty soon."

"Why? What's the hurry? Not like you've got any big family thing to get home to. Didn't you say it was just you and Judith yesterday?"

"I did. But I want to get home in time to eat some of those Thanksgiving leftovers before we head down to the Bass Pro Shop."

Barney cast his red spinnerbait out again. "I am starting to get a little hungry myself. How did Judith handle the kids not being home for Thanksgiving?"

"Not too well, I think. She was kind of mopey all day. I enjoyed it, though. All that peace and quiet for a change. Got to watch the football game without any interruptions. That's a first for a Thanksgiving." He tossed out another cast. "So what do you think, should we start wrapping up?"

"All right," Barney said. "But you're gonna give me a chance to catch up with you, aren't ya?"

"It'll be dark out before that happens."

"No, it won't. Not if we switch."

"What do you mean, switch?"

"Switch baits. You use my red spinner and let me use your new rattle bait. That way we can prove once and for all whether your 3–0 lead is because of your fishing skill or your new bait."

"You're on," Stan said and handed him his pole.

3

S tan came home smelling of fish. But Judith had come to think of that as a good thing. It meant he'd have some fish stories to tell. Not that she liked hearing them; by now they all rather sounded alike. But stories about catching fish were preferable to hearing about the ones that got away. It also meant he'd brought home fresh bass fillets to put in the freezer.

That was the rule—he cleaned the fish before he got home, and they had to be filleted. She didn't like fish skin or picking fish bones out of her mouth. Those things settled, Judith was okay with the fish and had even discovered some nice bass recipes. They still weren't the best-tasting fish, in her opinion, but they made for a passable meal.

Stan always liked to point out they were eating free food. And she would point out that after you added the fresh water licenses, the bait and tackle, the gas for the boat, the repairs for the boat, the bug spray and sunscreen, the bags of ice, and all the other miscellaneous expenses Stan didn't want to focus on, the food was no longer free.

Judith had figured out that these "free" bass fillets actually cost a tad more per pound than the finest cut of filet mignon. She kept that information to herself. Truth was, she was glad he'd found something he enjoyed so much. Hobbies and pastimes, on the whole, were a good thing. They added spice to your life and gave you something to look forward to in the midst of the monotony and mundane.

Her problem wasn't Stan's hobby; it was hers. Her kids and grandchildren. Now they were gone.

"You not feeling well?"

Judith looked up from the table. "What?"

"Your food. I'm almost done, and you've hardly touched a bite. Tastes better than yesterday, if you ask me."

She looked down at a slightly smaller version of yesterday's Thanksgiving feast. "I'm fine. I've eaten some."

"Not very much." He leaned back in his chair, looked around the living area and at the two boxes of Christmas decorations still on the dinette table. "Besides that, normally when I get home from fishing the day after Thanksgiving, you have the house all decorated for the holidays."

"And normally I'd have some help." She forked a piece of turkey, stirred it around in some gravy. She heard him sigh.

"Nothing much I can do about that," he said. He looked back at the boxes. "Doesn't look like you even started."

She set the fork down. "That's because I haven't."

"Are you planning on starting anytime soon? Barney's going to be over here in about ten minutes. If it's all right with you, we're still planning on heading down to the Bass Pro store in Orlando."

"I figured you would," she said.

"You still okay with that?"

"Why wouldn't I be? There's no reason you should change your plans on account of me." Judith realized as soon as she'd said it she was playing with his head a little. Opening the guilt door a few inches. But that wasn't what she wanted. It wasn't Stan's fault the kids had moved away. Anyway, there was no danger he'd feel guilty enough to cancel a trip to the Bass Pro Shop with Barney.

He scooped up his last forkful of mashed potatoes as she asked him, "You want some pumpkin pie?"

"Maybe you could put a slice on a paper plate? I can take it on the road."

"You said Barney wouldn't be here for ten minutes. You have time enough for pie, if you want it."

He slid his chair back from the table. "I still need to get the tree set up in the corner, then climb up to the attic and bring down those boxes of ornaments. Just in case you get your energy back."

Judith didn't see that happening. "I don't think energy's my problem. I'm just not in the mood. Besides, I don't see any reason to hurry on this stuff, just because we've always done it the day after Thanksgiving. It's not like there's going to be anybody here to see it but you and me."

Stan stood. "You're right. There's no law that says it's all got to go up today. But I'm still going up in the attic to bring those boxes down. Just in case your mood changes. If you don't get to it all today, you can finish it tomorrow." He started walking toward the garage.

Well, wasn't that nice of him, giving her another day to decorate. She noticed he didn't include helping her this year as an option. "Speaking of laws . . . there's no law that says you couldn't help me with some of this decorating." The door leading into the garage closed. She wasn't sure he'd even heard her.

She walked back to the table and took one more bite of turkey. But she was done eating what was on this plate. After walking back to the kitchen counter, she set it down and reached for the pumpkin pie. She cut two slices, figured she might just be interested in something sweet. She set Stan's on the paper plate and walked into the living room. She switched around an end table and a small upholstered chair in the corner, making a spot for the Christmas tree.

Stan would be bringing that in first. Then she remembered, she did need to open up one of the boxes of decorations, to get a Christmassy tablecloth out. Last year, they'd opted for a little four-foot artificial tree, one they'd bought for half off at Hobby Lobby. Stan especially liked the fact that it came with all the lights already wired in. All he had to do was stick the plug in the wall. But the tree was so short, they had to prop it up on an end table to make it the right height. She quickly found the bright red tablecloth, unfolded it, tossed it over the end table, and straightened it up.

"There," she said aloud. "That should do it."

A moment later the interior door to the garage banged open. That would be Stan, dragging in the tree. She watched as he came around the wall that separated the living room and the kitchen.

He looked toward the proper corner. "Good, it's all set

up." He glanced at his watch. "Barney's gonna be here any minute."

"Your pumpkin pie's on a paper plate on the counter."

"Saw it, thanks." He headed back toward the garage. "Time to get the ornaments down. I'm glad we got that shorter tree. Only three boxes to bring down this year." He disappeared into the kitchen.

They used to have five boxes when they set up a full-sized tree. She'd given two boxes to Suzanne when she moved to Fort Worth. She remembered that moment well. It wasn't a happy one. For Suzanne it was. She loved getting all those familiar ornaments for her family. But Judith knew that Suzanne would be hanging those ornaments on a tree in Texas.

A tree Judith would never see.

A few minutes later, the kitchen door banged open again. Stan carried the boxes of ornaments over to the coffee table and set them down. "Well, that should do it. That's everything." Then a look on his face. "Oops, almost forgot." He walked over to the tree, found the end of the plug, and pushed it into the wall. Several hundred little white lights instantly lit up. "There," he announced. "You're all set. If that doesn't get you in a Christmas mood, nothing will."

She was about to say, "Then I guess nothing will," but didn't. The lights on the tree were nice. But they did little to lift her spirits.

"Maybe you'd feel better if you broke tradition and hung the ornaments on the tree first. Set up the decorations around the house after."

She wanted to say, "You're kidding, right?" But she heard a horn beep in front of the house. "There's Barney. You better go, or he'll keep honking."

After giving her a peck on the cheek and grabbing his pie, he said, "See you in a few hours."

She walked over to the sparkling tree, then glanced at the three boxes of ornaments. She loved decorating the tree. But usually when accomplishing this task, Judith had several happy helpers.

This year she would be doing it by herself . . . if she did it at all.

4

For Stan, walking through the front doors of the Bass Pro Shop in Orlando was like being a kid walking down Main Street in Disney World. There was no place on earth he'd rather be. Judging by the look on his face, Barney felt the same way. And of course, with the place all done up for Christmas, the effect was tenfold.

As with most men, shopping was serious business to Stan. You figure out what you want before you get there, go right to the aisle, pick out the best value for the money, and head to the register. Lickety-split. No dillydallying.

But not here. Not at Bass Pro Shop.

Here, a man took his time. Savored the moment. Walked slowly. Took in the sights. And there were plenty of sights to see, everywhere he looked. The last time they had visited, Barney had said, "This must be what a woman feels like at the mall."

"Yep," Stan said. "Think you're right."

They were primarily here to look at the fishing department, but every part of the store held fascination and wonder. Stan had never hunted before but found himself curiously drawn to everything he saw on the shelves and hanging on the walls. Hunting and fishing did tend to go together, like that magazine *Field and Stream*. "Ever thought about hunting, Barney?"

Barney was staring at a rack of shotguns. "I hunted as a kid up in Michigan. Never did it once we moved down here to Florida."

"So you like fishing better then?"

"I guess," Barney said. "Not so much better, just different. Lots of good memories, hunting. I could see myself taking it up again someday. Don't see as I have time for both yet. Maybe when I'm fully retired." He lifted one of the shotguns off the rack, pretended to take aim. Then his eyes got real bright, seeing the old-fashioned shooting gallery nearby. He pointed to it with the gun. "What say we spend a few minutes over there and I teach you a thing or two about shootin'?"

Stan looked. "Might as well." What was a visit to Bass Pro Shop without spending time at the shooting gallery? It was like being a kid again.

On the way, Stan stopped a moment and pointed toward Santa's Wonderland, an entire section of the store transformed into a Bass Pro version of the North Pole. The place was filled with animated Christmas characters like reindeer and nutcrackers and Christmas elves. They had remote control trucks, a laser arcade, even slot car racing. And piles of fake snow all around like it had just fallen from the sky. "When we're done at the shooting gallery, let's go in there."

"The trains?"

Stan nodded. Maybe for the kids, the big reindeer carousel was the centerpiece of Santa's Wonderland, or the Big Guy himself if he was in the store. But for Stan it was the snow-covered Lionel train layout. Complete with an old-timey steam locomotive, an animated gondola, and a boxcar that played Christmas music. If you came at the right time, you could even man the controls.

Barney looked at his watch.

"What's the matter?" Stan said. "We got plenty of time."

"I know, but there's so much to look at in this place. Don't let me forget before we leave, I want to show you that new high-tech trolling motor I read about in the magazine. They got one here. We gotta put one of those on our dream rig."

Ah, Stan thought, the dream rig.

Finally, this was going to be the year—the year he and Barney purchased their dream bass fishing boat. He'd waited so long. Both of them had. But Stan had been raised right. You don't put your hobbies and toys ahead of your family's needs. When the kids lived at home, there was never enough money left over to save a single dime. So every year, he and Barney would sit in their old boat, watching other fishermen glide by in style.

But not anymore.

Now that his children were launched, pursuing their own lives and growing their own families, it was just him and Judith. He'd started saving for that boat right away. And now, finally, it was going to be his turn.

"Earth to Stan, Earth to Stan."

Stan focused on Barney's face.

"I was talking about this new high-tech trolling motor I want to show you."

"I thought our dream rig already came with a trolling motor," Stan said.

"It does. But it's just a basic one. For a dream rig, you need a dream trolling motor. This one'll cost more, but it's well worth it. Wait till you see what it can do. It's totally wireless, works with a remote control you can operate with one hand. Got its own GPS system, so you can fix on a certain spot, get the boat there, then the trolling motor will keep you there while you fish. You drift a little, it'll take you right back. And because it's electric, it operates silently, so it won't scare away the fish."

Stan had to admit, he liked the sound of that. But their dream rig was already up to ten thousand dollars. And that wasn't for a new boat, just a good used one. They were just weeks away now. The guy they had been talking with said he'd hold it for them until Christmas with a five-hundred-dollar, nonrefundable deposit. After that, he said he couldn't wait anymore. The boat they had been fishing in for the last several years was a total embarrassment. Both of them hated it, but very soon their shame would be over.

"So what do you think?" Barney said.

"I think we should go see this thing before we leave. But I also think we might need to wait on buying something so fancy till after the New Year, especially since the new boat already comes with a trolling motor. It will take every penny we can scrimp together between now and Christmas to close the gap on that ten thousand dollars."

"Aren't you forgetting something?" Barney said.

"I don't think so."

"How much you think we're going to get when we sell our old boat and trailer?"

"We'd be lucky to get five hundred."

"That's about what I figured." They'd just reached the shooting gallery. "We get our ten thousand figure nailed down, then you add five hundred dollars more for our old boat. Did you factor that in?"

Stan had not.

"Well, there you go. That's where the money's gonna come from for this new trolling motor." He walked over toward an empty gun station at the shooting gallery, picked up the rifle.

Stan smiled. He hadn't thought about that. After walking toward the station next to Barney, he bent over and picked up his rifle.

"Five dollars says I beat you by more than ten points," Barney said.

"You're on." Then Stan thought of something. "I need to go use the restroom first."

"That's not going to help your aim any."

Stan laughed. "No, but it will help my concentration. Tell you what, I'm so confident of winning that bet, you can practice while I'm gone."

"I think I will."

Stan set the rifle back in its holder and headed toward the restroom. On the way there, his phone rang. He stopped to answer it. It was Betty, Barney's wife. Why would she be calling him? She and Judith were close friends, though not as close as Stan and Barney. "Hey, Betty, did you mean to call Barney? Did he leave his phone volume off?"

"No, Stan. I called you on purpose. I was just on Facebook uploading some Thanksgiving pics from our family time yesterday. Expected to see some from Judith, but there weren't any. So I called her to see how she was doing, and she didn't answer the phone. Is she okay?"

"She's probably just busy decorating the tree or putting up decorations in the house," Stan said. "She's having to do it all herself this year."

"Why's that?"

"None of the kids came home. It was just the two of us."

"Really? The poor thing."

Stan was about to say how he'd rather enjoyed it but held his peace.

"She must be feeling something awful," Betty said.

"She did seem a little down when I left with Barney to come here."

"I'm gonna try to call her again."

Stan waited, wondering if Betty had anything more to say. Didn't seem like she did. "Well, guess I'll get back to shopping with Barney. Appreciate you calling her."

They hung up, and Stan headed for the restroom.

5

Judith had just gotten off the phone with Betty, who had invited herself over for a visit. She was on her way here now. Judith wasn't sure she was up for company, but it was nice of her to come. Betty had mentioned talking with Stan on the phone. For a moment, Judith entertained the thought that Stan had noticed how sad she was and asked Betty to call. Then another thought came: *When pigs fly*.

Walking to the kitchen, Judith took inventory of her situation. She had the energy to put on a fresh pot of coffee for Betty, but that was it. That and the pumpkin pie. She had already finished the slice she had eaten after Stan left. That was almost two hours ago. It was high time for another. That pie had been the closest she'd come to feeling joy all day. Perhaps a bigger slice would cause the sensation to last a little longer.

She set the coffee brewing and put the pie slices on dessert plates. An image flashed into her mind, causing a glance toward the boxes of Christmas decorations on the table. Should she bother? She had a set of Christmas plates in one of those containers. She'd purchased them in one of Mount Dora's downtown antique shops about ten years ago. Genuine Jamestown china, the saleswoman had said, as if that should mean something. Judith had just fallen in love with the holly-berry pattern, and they were surprisingly affordable.

Why not? She fetched the pie plates out of the container and carried them to the opposite end of the table. A moment later, Betty's car pulled into the driveway.

Judith was suddenly aware of how quiet the house was. Maybe she should turn on the radio. Her favorite FM station started playing Christmas music the day after Thanksgiving. She walked up to the radio, then changed her mind. She wasn't in a Christmas mood, not even close. No sense pretending for Betty's sake.

Instead, she walked back to the kitchen and checked on the coffee's progress. The last few drips were making their way into the pot. As she pulled a couple of mugs out of the cabinet, the doorbell rang.

"Come on in, Betty," she yelled through the open windows. "It's unlocked." The screen door then the front door both opened and closed. "I'm in here, just getting the coffee ready." Judith knew how Betty liked it. "There are two slices of pie sitting on the table."

"My goodness, Judith. They're both way too big."

"Well, just eat what you can."

"Oh, I'm gonna eat the whole thing. But it wouldn't be right if I didn't complain."

Judith laughed. Betty could always make her laugh. She poured the coffee and brought the mugs out.

"Are we supposed to eat this pie with our hands? I'm okay with that. It'll still taste the same."

"I'm sorry," Judith said. "I'm not thinking straight today." She walked back to the kitchen and grabbed some forks.

"A little birdy told me you were feeling kind of down."

Judith handed her a fork, then sat by the other slice of pie.

"Judging by these unopened containers lying around here with 'Christmas' written on the sides and that Christmas tree over there in the corner without any ornaments, I'm guessing you're having a little trouble getting in the Christmas spirit."

Judith nodded and continued chewing. When she finished, she said, "I suppose I'll get there eventually. I'm guessing you got your decorating done already."

Betty finished a sip of coffee. "Got most of it done on Monday. Like we always do. The first day of Thanksgiving week. Our family likes to see the house all done up by Thanksgiving dinner."

"That's nice."

Betty seemed to realize what she'd said. "I'm sorry, put my foot in it, didn't I? That's what's eating you. None of the kids coming home yesterday."

Judith nodded, ate another forkful of pie.

"No, none of them made it home yesterday, and now . . ." She didn't mean to, but she started choking up. "Now none of them are able to make it home for Christmas either."

Betty reached over and patted the top of her hand. "Hence, the oversized slices of pie," she said.

Judith smiled, took another bite, then looked up at Betty. "I hope you understand, I'm not jealous of you having all your family home and around the dinner table yesterday. I'm glad you and Barney got to do that, and that y'all got to make another year of memories, especially with your grandkids."

"I know that, Judith."

She looked down at what was left of her pie. "It was just so hard having me and Stan at the table by ourselves. The time just crawled by. Instead of laughter and listening to the grandkids' stories and updates, the most memorable sound was Stan's fork clanking on the plate."

"I'm sorry." Just then, Betty's fork clanked on the plate. "For that too."

Judith scooped up her last bite of pie. "I was comforting myself with the notion that at least I had Christmas to look forward to. Then after I talked with the kids on the phone, that got ripped away too."

Betty sipped her coffee. "You know what the problem is, don't you? You and Stan pushed your kids a tad too hard in school, and then you went and set aside all that money for college. They got smart and became successful. And your daughters married successful college graduates. They all got good jobs but had to move to bigger cities."

Judith smiled. Give Betty an A for effort. The truth was, Judith had actually wondered the very same thing yesterday— during one of those long, dull moments sitting alone with Stan at the table. Betty had joked like this before, pointing out how educated and successful Judith's kids were. As if Betty were jealous. The truth was, Betty's kids were anything but dumb and they all seemed pretty successful.

Today, Judith felt like the joke was on her.

6

After they ate their pie, Judith poured them both another cup of coffee, and they moved into the living room. Betty glanced at the tree, barren except for the lights, then at the three boxes stacked on the coffee table. "I'm guessing these are the ornaments?"

"What's left of them," Judith said. She spun the boxes around so the handwritten label could be seen from the couch. "We used to have two more, bigger than these, back when we had a full-sized tree. I gave those to Suzanne when she moved to Fort Worth. I kept all the ornaments I really cared about."

Betty leaned toward the boxes. "What's that say?" She pointed to the middle one. "The Ugly Ornaments? What in the world is that?"

"Stan wrote that. That's what he likes to call them."

"Why are they ugly? And if they are, why do you keep them?"

Judith lifted the top box off the stack and set it on the table. "Open it. See for yourself." Betty opened the box, revealing a number of small packages wrapped in newspaper.

"Are they fragile?" Betty asked. "I don't want to break any of them."

"Some are. But you should be all right if you just use a little care. I mostly wrapped them to keep them from getting tangled, and to keep the paint from scratching off."

Betty lifted two of them out. "Oh my." She was unwrapping the first one. "Now that's ugly."

Judith smiled. Betty was holding up one that Brandon had made. If Judith remembered right, when he was eight years old.

"It looks like a shrunken head," Betty said. "Is that what it's supposed to be?"

Judith laughed. "No. Why would we ever make shrunken heads as Christmas ornaments?"

"What's it supposed to be then?" She spun it slowly around with her fingers as it dangled from a hook.

"It's supposed to be a Christmas elf."

"Where's its body?"

"It's just supposed to be his head. But he's supposed to have a little green hat on. It must've fallen off in the box."

"Did it ever look like a Christmas elf? Maybe when you first made it?" Betty handed it to her as she opened up the next one.

"I think it's always looked like a shrunken head," Judith said. "And I didn't make it. Brandon did. The kids made all of these when they were little. I helped them. I came up

31

with most of the ideas, bought all the little craft supplies. But the kids put them all together." She spun the shrunken elf head around. "Of course, none of them turned out like they were supposed to."

Betty opened the second one. "What is *this* supposed to be?"

"Aww," Judith said softly. She gently set the elf down on the table and reached for the ornament Betty was holding now. "Suzanne made that when she was six. There should be another one in there nearby. Anna made one too. Hers was a little nicer. She was three years older."

"Okay, but what is it? I know it's not what I think it is."

"What does it look like to you?"

"It looks like . . . a shrieking ghost . . . with jaundice and a bad complexion."

Judith laughed and tried to see what Betty was seeing. "It's supposed to be a Christmas caroler singing with her eyes closed. Like in Dickens's time. See the lacy collar? We made the heads by hollowing out eggs and spraying them with some kind of finish. I don't remember now what it was called. Then the kids painted them, trying to make it look like skin. Suzanne didn't like how hers turned out, so she kept adding more coats with different colors."

"There's another one in here?" Betty said, looking in the box.

"Another girl is in there somewhere. The one Anna made. It came out much better. Well, a little better. But I think we lost the one Brandon made, or else it broke a few years ago. Believe it or not, it looked even worse than the one you're holding. Stan thought it looked like a vampire."

Betty handed the Christmas caroler to Judith and reached

for another. As she unwrapped it, she laughed out loud. "I'm sorry. I don't mean to make fun. But this one . . ." She held it up for Judith to see. "You don't want to know what I think this looks like."

Judith could guess. It was probably the same thing Stan had said about it whenever they'd put it on the tree. He even had a nickname for it. Brandon had made the ornament when he was nine. When he was younger, he used to get upset whenever Stan made fun of it. But the last few Christmases, Brandon had laughed just as hard when he saw it hanging on the tree. "I think I know what you think it looks like. Just go ahead and say it."

"It looks like . . . dog poop."

They both laughed. It really did. "It's supposed to be a little Christmas tree."

"I'm not seeing a Christmas tree . . . anywhere," Betty said.

"It used to be more green years ago. And all the colorful little ornament thingies Brandon glued on have fallen off."

"I see," Betty said.

"Stan always called it the poop ornament." Looking at it now, Judith wondered if it ever really looked like anything else.

Betty unwrapped another one. "Well, this one's kind of cute."

Judith looked. Betty was holding a little larger ornament made of pipe cleaners mostly, spray painted pink.

"It's the Pink Panther, right?" Betty said.

"A flamingo."

"Oh." Betty looked at it again. "Okay, a flamingo then."

"Stan surprised us and took us to Sea World that year. The kids loved the flamingos."

Betty unwrapped another and held up two longish, green ornaments. "Caterpillars?" she said.

"Pickles," Judith said. "We made them by cutting green socks in half and stuffing them with cotton balls."

Betty smiled. "Nice. Christmas pickles." She set them down next to the others on the coffee table. "Is the whole box full of . . . ornaments just like these?"

"Pretty much," Judith said. "They started getting a little better as the kids got older. I'm not sure what year we started, though. I don't think Suzanne was even in kindergarten yet. But it became a fun tradition. Every year we'd make three of them, one for each child. And they'd proudly hang them on the tree. Then we'd carefully wrap them back up after the holiday until the next Christmas. As the years went by, we created quite a collection."

"When did you stop making them?"

"Before you and I even met. When the kids became teenagers, we did it for a few more years, but I could tell they had lost interest. They still loved hanging them on the tree, even more than all the fancy store-bought ornaments. And each time they unwrapped one of the ornaments they had made, they'd hang it on the tree and I'd ask them what they remembered about the day we made them. We'd have the best time recalling all the fun we had when they were little."

Judith looked down at the table. They had continued that tradition every year until . . . now. This would be the first year the kids weren't here to hang the ugly ornaments on the tree. This would be the year the tradition died. The thought of that brought tears to her eyes. She quickly blinked them away and began wrapping the ornaments back up in the paper and setting them back inside the box.

"Don't you want to put them on the tree?" Betty said. "They already have hooks."

"No. I don't. All these years, I've never hung a single one of these ornaments. The kids did. I don't think I can start doing it now."

7

About an hour after Betty arrived, Judith could tell she was getting ready to leave. She was sitting on the edge of the cushion, glancing at the clock on the wall, talking about all the things she had to accomplish before the afternoon was over. Meanwhile, the Christmas decorations still sat in their containers on the dining room table. The bare Christmas tree still stood in the corner. And the ornaments still sat in the three boxes on the coffee table.

About twenty minutes ago, Betty had asked if she could turn on that FM radio station, let some Christmas music into the room. Judith said sure. She'd be moving into Scrooge territory if she said no. But listening to it had the opposite effect on Judith than Betty probably intended.

"Do you realize that's the second time that station has played 'Rockin' Around the Christmas Tree' since you turned it on?" Judith said. "That's the only thing I don't like about this station. Every year they play the same stupid songs, over and over again. Just wait, they've already played 'Jingle Bell Rock' once. A few minutes from now, they'll play it again. Twenty minutes later, they'll play it again."

Betty joined in. "They'll probably play 'The Little Drummer Boy' again too. They play that one all the time. Now, that's got to be the dumbest Christmas song ever. 'Shall I play for you?' Uh, no, I just got the baby Jesus asleep. The last thing we need in this stable is some kid banging on a drum."

Judith laughed. "I don't recall ever seeing a little drummer boy on a nativity set."

"Or reading about one showing up that night in the Bible," Betty added.

As soon as she'd said that, "Santa Baby" began playing on the radio. Judith nodded her head to the intro, then mouthed the words along with Eartha Kitt.

Betty stood up and turned the radio off. "This isn't helping the cause. Who puts these song lists together anyway? They need to let people like you and me do it."

Judith wondered why she'd ever liked listening to that station in past years. She noticed Betty remained standing.

"I'm sorry you're having such a bad day," Betty said. "I don't know if me coming over here helped anything or made matters worse."

"Oh, it's definitely helped. I appreciate you trying, Betty. I'm sure I'll get over this after a while." Judith said this without an ounce of confidence.

"I think I know something that'll help for sure. Why don't you come downtown with me tomorrow afternoon to do some shopping? You know how pretty they make the downtown area the Saturday after Thanksgiving. They pull out all the stops. I was driving through there this morning. Things are already getting set up for it. We can go shopping for a couple hours, maybe start at two thirty or so. Then have the boys join us for a quick bite to eat around five. Right after that, they have the big Light Up ceremony at Donnelly Park."

Judith remembered. When the kids and grandkids were here, they never missed it. The whole town gathered together in the downtown area, and just when it got dark, they'd flip the switch and over two million lights would spring to life. Mount Dora might be a small town, but they really knew how to do Christmas right. Judith had never visited a single big-city Christmas display that impressed her more. "That might be nice," she said.

"Can I come by and pick you up?" Betty said. "About two fifteen?"

"Sure."

"Stan better let you have some money to spend."

He would, but how much was another question.

"Tell you what," Betty continued, "get him to show you that receipt he brings home from the Bass Pro Shop today. And you tell him I said you get to spend at least that much with me tomorrow." Betty moved toward the front door.

"I will," Judith said.

"Thanks again for the coffee and pie. Wish I could say I was going to go work it off, but that ain't happening."

They hugged and Betty headed for her car.

It was just a little before five when Stan arrived home. There was no doubt about it, it had been a very fun day.

Perfect weather in the morning for fishing, skunked Barney three bass to zero, had the most amazing time at the Bass Pro Shop. Some killer deals on tackle and other outdoor supplies, not to mention all the fun with the Lionel trains and the shooting gallery.

He'd convinced Barney they should hold off buying that fancy trolling motor until after they'd actually sold their fishing boat. But he had agreed with Barney that it was the finest trolling motor he'd ever seen and definitely deserved a rightful place on their dream rig.

Stan paused in front of their little house. Barney had been in a bit of a hurry, so he'd dropped Stan off on the street rather than pulling in the driveway. Stan thought about some of the fancier homes he'd seen out on the water this morning and decided he liked their place just fine. It was all they really needed at this point. And it was fixed up just the way they liked it, which meant less time for chores and more time for fishing.

The house had a nice picket fence across the front made of pressure-treated wood, so it didn't need painting. All the plants they had picked out, both along the fence and closer to the house, were low-maintenance types. Ones that could withstand the occasional winter freeze, which towns in central Florida were known to have once in a while. They lived on an oversized lot with an abundance of trees, providing plenty of shade and privacy. The shady trees did a number on the lawn, though, since most kinds of grass needed plenty of sunshine to thrive. That didn't bother Stan any; it meant he had less grass to mow.

He walked around the picket fence and came into the driveway, intending to go in the side door, through the kitchen. This was the angle of the house he enjoyed the most. The late afternoon sun came through the trees in such a way that it really brightened up the burnt-red clapboard siding and the stand-alone garage at the end of the driveway. It dawned on him . . . with the redness of the house and all the green trees and shrubs surrounding it, he really didn't need to decorate the outside much for Christmas. The house was already decorated in Christmas colors year-round.

In previous years, he couldn't get that argument to fly with Judith, or with his kids.

They'd decorate the inside of the house so much, they'd want the outside to match. It wasn't so bad when his son Brandon still lived at home. He could do most of the ladder work and heavy lifting. Even with his help, it still took the better part of an afternoon.

As Stan made his way down the driveway, he realized . . . this year he might catch a break after all. None of the kids were coming home. He did it for them mostly. He never put up enough lights to compete with the fanatics.

He opened the door and stepped into the kitchen. When he smelled the turkey leftovers heating up, it brought back a fond memory. But then he noticed that the other half of that memory was missing.

There was no Christmas music playing. No Christmas decorations lining the shelves and countertops. He walked through the kitchen, saw the two containers on the dining room table, right where he'd left them. Looked into the living room. No Christmas decorations in there either. No ornaments on the tree. The three boxes still sat there on the coffee table.

And no Judith.

"Judith?" he yelled. No answer. He walked into the living room. "Judith?"

8

I'm out here, Stan."

Stan walked through the French doors he'd installed when they'd added on the Florida room nine years ago. Typically people built these rooms onto the back of the house, but Stan had to build his on the side, due to the way the house was laid out. On the upside, lots of windows faced a well-shaded and private side yard. Judith sat in an upholstered chair staring out one of those windows. "You gave me a little scare there."

Without shifting her gaze, she said, "Did you think I ran off?"

"No. Well . . . I didn't know what to think." He took a few steps toward her. "Just getting back from Orlando."

She didn't reply. Just kept looking out the window.

"Smells good, what you're heating up in the kitchen."

"It should be ready to eat. Help yourself. You know where the plates and silverware are."

"Aren't you going to join me?"

"I had two slices of pumpkin pie this afternoon. Guess I spoiled my dinner. But you go ahead."

"You mean . . . eat alone?"

"Well, I guess I do. You've been out all afternoon. I'm sure you worked up an appetite. I'm just not hungry." She still hadn't looked at him.

He stood there a few more moments, not sure what to say. "Did Betty call you?"

"She did. Even came over for a while."

He wanted to say, "Did it help any?" But it was clear Betty's visit hadn't helped. He stood there a few moments more. "Can I get you anything?"

"No, thank you."

So formal. If anything, she seemed worse than when he'd left her this afternoon. With nothing left to do, Stan turned and headed back to the kitchen. He was hungry, after all, and the food was ready. He fixed a plate that pretty much resembled what he'd eaten yesterday and sat alone at the dining room table. Thanksgiving dinner tasted even better the next day.

As much as he enjoyed the food, he didn't enjoy eating alone. Was she mad at him? Had he done something wrong? He'd only done what he did every other day-after-Thanksgiving for as many years as he could remember. This was his tradition.

But Judith hadn't followed through with hers. Not one bit of it.

Stan finished his meal, still puzzling over the situation, still sitting at the dining room table. He tried to remember what the house should look like about now. Though he rarely participated in the actual decorating, he'd always been impressed with how wonderful their home looked when Judith and the kids were done. They'd really go all out. Every flat surface in every room would reflect some kind of Christmas cheer. He didn't know how many Christmas decorations she would set out. At least dozens.

They had been married for forty years, and they'd lived all that time in Mount Dora, a town known for extravagant holiday traditions. Every year, Judith would go shopping downtown a few days after Christmas, when the stores would slash prices, and add a few new items to her collection. When Judith and the kids would finish decorating their home, it would be on par with the kind of Christmas spirit you'd see on display throughout the town.

Well, that was how the house *usually* looked. Today it looked just like it did every other day.

Stan stood and walked his plate, silverware, and glass to the counter by the sink. That was usually as far as he went with it. Today, he rinsed things off and actually set them in the dishwasher. He looked at the rest of the food still sitting out. They weren't expecting any company. "Hey, Judith," he yelled, "sure you don't want to fix yourself a plate?" He hoped she'd say yes. He really didn't want to have to put everything away.

She didn't answer.

He walked back toward the doorway leading into the Florida room. "Are you hungry yet?"

She was back to staring out the window, but she looked up and released a sigh. "Still not hungry. But don't worry about it. I'll get up in a little while and put everything away."

"You're not going to eat anything?"

"I may eat a few pieces of turkey later. But don't worry about it."

He stood there a moment. Her eyes shifted from him back to the spot in the side yard she had been staring at before. "You going to just sit there all night?"

"No. Not all night."

"Are you going to do anything with these decorations, the ones on the table? Or these boxes of ornaments?"

"I suppose so, eventually. Not in the mood right now."

"Well, how about the Christmas movie? Still want to do that tonight?" That had been their end-of-the-day, day-after-Thanksgiving tradition. Watch a movie together. The house all decorated. The leftovers all served. The food put away. The dishes done. Then everyone would gather in the living room to eat dessert and watch a Christmas movie. Not always the same one each year. They'd vote between a few that the family considered classics: *It's a Wonderful Life*, *A Christmas Carol*, *A Christmas Story*. In recent years, *Elf* had been added to the ranks.

"Maybe," she said. "In a little while."

"Since it's just you and me, we won't vote. I'll let you pick which one."

"Right, just you and me. No need to vote."

Okay, that kinda backfired. Slowly, he walked toward her and sat on the edge of the matching upholstered chair, trying to think of something to say. Nothing came. She glanced his way but didn't say anything either. He had never seen her like this before. Generally, if one of them was silent, it was him.

Finally she said, "I've realized something. Without the kids, I have no purpose in life."

"What? That's not true. You've got all kinds of purpose."

"Like what? Name one thing I do that's important or essential. One thing I do that makes a difference."

All kinds of things started popping off in his head. Keep the house. Cook the meals. Buy the food. Do the laundry. Keep their schedule straight. Remember birthdays and anniversaries, for their kids and grandkids. And there were probably lots of other things he wasn't thinking of. They all seemed important to him, but he knew they weren't things she'd consider important or essential.

"See," she said, "you know it's true."

"No, I don't. I don't think it, because it isn't true. You do all kinds of important things. Maybe they're not *absolutely* essential in the big scheme of life, but they're certainly things that matter to us. Things that keep life running fairly smooth around here. If you didn't buy the food and cook it, we'd starve. If you didn't clean the clothes, we'd start to stink and look like bums."

She smiled. It wasn't a big one, but it was something.

"I'm not talking about things like that," she said. "I know they matter in their own way. Maybe I should've said the word *meaningful*. I don't do anything meaningful, anything that makes a real difference. I've been so focused on our kids and grandkids for so many years. With them out of the picture, there goes my purpose in life. I'm not even a part-time mom or grandmother anymore. And now, not even on holidays."

Stan didn't know what to say. He thought she sounded a

little bit like Jimmy Stewart's character George Bailey in *It's a Wonderful Life*. In the movie, George was at his wit's end and thought the world would be better off if he had never been born. Stan was about to suggest they should watch that movie tonight. But then he realized that movie had a happy ending and George Bailey got all kinds of help from an angel named Clarence.

Stan didn't have that kind of help here tonight. And he sure didn't have any idea how to turn this dilemma into a happy ending.

9

On Saturday afternoon, Judith wasn't doing any better. If anything, she awoke that morning to a greater sense of gloom than she'd experienced before bed last night. It probably didn't help that Stan had gotten called into work early that morning, which meant she'd been alone all day.

Of course, it wasn't as if Stan being there would've made all that much difference. He wasn't exactly a Grade-A conversationalist. But his absence accentuated the emptiness she felt inside. She walked over and sat on the sofa, glanced up at the clock on the wall. Betty would be here in a few minutes to take her on their promised shopping excursion downtown. The plan was for the men to join them at five for a bite to eat. Then they'd join the throng gathering around Donnelly Park to watch them turn the Christmas lights on all over town.

She wasn't sure that part of the plan would work anymore. Stan said before he left that he had been scheduled to work until four today. But they were so busy, all bets were off now. He said he'd text her when he knew something sure.

She glanced down at the three boxes of ornaments on the coffee table in front of her and read the label of the box on top. She couldn't help but smile as she reread the label Stan had written: The Ugly Ornaments. She lifted the lid and pulled out the few sitting on top, the ones Betty had opened yesterday when she was here. Judith wanted to see the kids' favorites once again. They had made all of them over many years, but somehow each of the kids had managed to pick a favorite. One they liked more than all the rest.

Judith had her own favorites, but they weren't the same ones the kids had picked. Hers, you could say, were the least ugly ones in the box. She pulled the box closer and began taking out more ornaments and setting them on the coffee table, leaving them wrapped. She had stored the kids' favorites in bright green wrapping paper to make them easier to find.

In a few moments, she'd found all three. She hesitated before unwrapping them. Each one contained so many memories. She picked up the largest of the three, knowing whose it was by its size. Anna's blue pinecone. She unwrapped it.

They'd had such fun the day seven-year-old Anna had made it, and she'd been so proud. It turned out just the way she'd hoped. It was an oversized pinecone to start with, which meant it would always be relegated to the lower boughs of the Christmas tree. But that was okay, because in those early years, that was as far as Anna could reach. Judith's idea had been to spray paint it green, like a miniature Christmas tree.

She had little red plastic beads that Anna could glue on to serve as tiny ornaments.

That was the plan anyway.

But Anna's favorite color back then, and for many years after, was light blue. So she wanted her pinecone to be light blue. Judith had only bought green spray paint. Anna reminded her she had some light blue paint left over in a jar from a previous art project at school. She was so eager and excited about the prospect that Judith couldn't say no. Of course, the light blue came out all splotchy from being dabbed on with a brush by a seven-year-old.

Then Anna became impatient and wasn't willing to let the paint dry before gluing on the little red beads. Judith had left her alone at the table for a few minutes to check on dinner. When she returned, Anna had already glued on half of them. The red beads had light blue paint all over them and globs of Elmer's glue too. But Anna didn't mind. "Look, Mom!" she had said. "I'm almost done."

Judith had let her finish, and the end result was sitting before her now on the coffee table. My, my . . . it was a sight to behold. She slid it to one side, pulled one of the other two ornaments near, and unwrapped it. "Look at that," she said aloud.

It was Brandon's skeleton snowman. That was the nickname it had acquired over the years. Originally, it was bright white but now was a pale shade of yellow. Brandon had followed her directions carefully when making it. They never could quite figure out what went wrong. The idea was to form two doughnuts out of salt dough, one bigger than the other, to create the snowman's body. Then they rolled up a little dough ball to make its head. They layered the three sections on top of each other, and she let Brandon poke little holes with a toothpick in the front for buttons. With the same toothpick, he poked holes in the head to make eyes, a nose, and a smile. They baked it in the oven for two hours to harden everything up.

At some point, the whole thing had shifted sideways like the Leaning Tower of Pisa, and two cracks opened up in the back. The holes Brandon made in the head expanded a little, which changed the snowman's expression . . . a lot. It really did resemble a skull. Hence, the nickname "the skeleton snowman."

Judith had attempted to console him, suggesting they try again. But Brandon didn't care. He liked it just the way it was. And over time, it had become his favorite.

She reached for the third wrapped ornament, already knowing what it was. Suzanne's alien nativity set. The most disturbing one of all. It wasn't an entire nativity set, just Joseph, Mary, and baby Jesus. Well, that had been the idea. Judith unwrapped it and shook her head as she gazed at the horrific faces her little eight-year-old Suzanne had unintentionally painted on the figurines.

The original design idea was very cute. Three little figures, different sizes. Very simple. They reminded Judith of little Fisher-Price people made of wood instead of plastic. Little pieces of blue burlap were wrapped around Mary and Joseph, then glued on to serve as clothes. A little white cloth over Mary's head served as a scarf. Then Jesus was angled sideways against Mary and Joseph and glued to make it look like they were holding him.

They were only supposed to paint the heads a light peach color and leave it at that. But Suzanne had insisted they needed to have faces, and she wanted to paint them. Wanting to encourage creativity, Judith agreed. But when Suzanne was done, the faces didn't look right. It took Judith a moment to figure out what they reminded her of: space aliens. The face that everyone always associates with extraterrestrial beings: great big dark eyes, two dots for a nose, and a tiny sliver for a mouth.

Judith didn't want to make her feel bad, so she didn't say anything. When Stan got home, Suzanne proudly showed him her achievement, and he laughed out loud. "They look like aliens." Suzanne had shouted back, "No, they don't!" and ran to her room.

But they did.

And, of course, that was what they had been called ever since. Even Suzanne, a few years later, had been able to laugh along with everyone else every time she hung it on the tree.

Judith sighed.

That wouldn't happen this year. Suzanne was not here to hang her alien nativity ornament on the tree. Brandon would not hang his skeleton snowman. And Anna wouldn't hang her blue pinecone either.

Memories. That was what Christmastime meant to her. Recalling wonderful family times and creating new ones.

Judith wrapped all three of the ornaments up, set them back in the box, and closed the lid.

10

Betty had just arrived to pick Judith up. As she came into the living room, she looked around. "Guess you never got in the mood to do your Christmas decorations yesterday?"

Judith walked toward the front door. "Nope, never did."

"Hopefully that'll change once we hang out downtown a little while. I drove up Donnelly Avenue on my way here. It looks wonderful. The Christmas decorations are already up." Betty followed Judith out to the car.

They drove down the road back toward Donnelly Avenue, the main road that would take them to the center of town. The neighborhood was filled with shady trees and smaller, older homes like hers. And Judith loved the hills. Almost the entire state of Florida was absolutely flat. You could drive in some parts of the state for hours and the only elevation you'd see was a highway overpass.

Not in Mount Dora. Mount Dora had plenty of hills.

They were driving down one now as they approached Donnelly Avenue. Judith smiled as she thought of the town's name. *Mount* Dora. She read somewhere that the highest point in the city was 184 feet above sea level. A virtual mountaintop in Florida. They sold T-shirts to tourists downtown that said "I Climbed Mount Dora." It was meant to be a joke, but as she got older, Judith found that getting around certain parts of the downtown area was a true test of strength.

Betty turned left, and in a few minutes they were approaching downtown. "As you might expect, it's pretty crowded now. Saturdays are always more crowded, but this being the first official weekend for Christmas shopping, it's even worse. We're probably going to have to do some walking."

"I expected that," Judith said. "As long as we stay in the center of town and don't wander down by the lake. It's not the going down part, it's the climbing back up."

"I'm with you there." Betty turned left down one of the side streets. "I usually find a parking place pretty easily if I come one street back."

Sure enough, they found an open spot on Baker Street near the intersection with 5th Avenue. Judith was glad. They were only a block away from the stores. It was a beautiful day out, which brightened her mood somewhat. In between the trees, she felt the warmth of the sun on her arms. That was the thing about winters in central Florida; they could be chilly one year and mild the next. Really, it could be that way on any given week, which was why she always carried a sweater or light jacket whenever she went out. Right now she had a sweater slung over her arm.

They walked slightly downhill past Donnelly Park, the

Community Building on her right. She had been to so many events there over the years. Looked like something was going on right now. The Community Building was where the big Light Up ceremony would take place in a few hours.

As they neared the corner steps, she could already see the thousands of Christmas lights strung up through the park trees. She remembered from previous years just how amazing it was when they first turned them on. And they'd turn on lights up and down the streets of the downtown area. It made her proud to be a citizen of such a wonderful place.

Mount Dora had changed so little since she and Stan had moved here forty years ago, which was a large part of its charm. They had fallen in love with it on their first visit, in their first year of marriage. Both of them had been born up north but had moved to Florida as young children, so they'd always felt like native Floridians. Their parents had moved them, about a year apart, to the Tampa Bay area, which was where she and Stan had spent their middle and high school years. Tampa was a much bigger city, the third largest in the state.

When they drove through Mount Dora on that first trip, the town instantly reminded them of the small towns they remembered as children up north . . . complete with large shady trees and rolling hills. And the quaint little downtown area . . . it was perfect. Like something out of the 1950s. They decided right then and there, this was where they wanted to move and raise their kids.

Judith had thought her children loved small-town life as much as she and Stan did. When they were younger, they seemed very happy and talked about living here forever. But now, as she stood at the intersection waiting for the light to change, she wondered . . . did her kids still feel that way? How could they? All three of them now lived in big cities.

She felt Betty tug on her arm. She looked up.

"We can walk now."

"Oh." She hurried across the street, along with a small crowd of fellow shoppers.

"Where were you just now?" Betty asked. "Judging by the look on your face, it wasn't a fun place."

"You don't want to know." They stepped up onto the side-walk. "Besides, that's why we're here, right? To get my mind in a better place?"

Betty was determined to cheer her friend up. She had never seen Judith so down. She understood why. Well, she couldn't really understand; her kids and grandkids had been all around the dinner table on Thanksgiving. Same as every year. But she could imagine.

The downtown area was quite crowded. Everyone seemed to be in a good mood, so that helped. And of course, every building, every store window, even the streetlights were deco-rated for Christmas. She glanced over at Judith as they walked past the first store. Something had definitely caught her eye in the window. "You want to go in?"

"Sure."

Betty walked up to her. "What did you see?"

"Oh, there's all kinds of nice things in this store."

"I thought I saw you looking at one thing in particular."

"It was just this little Christmas town display here." She pointed to it. "I always thought about doing one of these.

Collecting all these little houses and buildings. I especially like the ones that move."

"Like those little ice-skaters?" Betty asked.

"Yes. And look at that little snowy mountain, with the skiers going down."

It really was cute. "Let's go inside. There are even more."

In the store, the collection expanded down the far wall a ways. "Look at this one, Judith. Miniature kids making snow angels. And right behind those little trees, see the kids in the snow playing tug-of-war." Betty watched Judith's eyes. It was working. She was beginning to enjoy herself.

"Look up on that hill," Judith said. "Three little boys all bundled up, gathered around a fire."

It was just precious. The little logs flickered with yellow and orange lights, as if they were on fire. The boys held their gloved hands forward, as if being warmed by the flames. "I love all the buildings too. You have to look in the windows, especially the ones lit up. There's all kinds of things happening inside them. Like this bakery. Look at all the little Christmas desserts in the storefront window."

Judith bent over to see.

"Which one is your favorite?" Betty asked. "Of all the ones here."

"Oh, I don't know. I like so many of them."

"Well, pick two that you'd really like. We can start your collection today. You buy one, and I'll buy the other. It'll be an early Christmas present."

Judith straightened up. "No, I can't do that."

"Sure you can. What's stopping you?"

"Look how much space they take up. Where would I put them if I started collecting them?"

"You've got all kinds of space in that big Florida room. We could move a few things around, free up one of the corners."

For a moment, just a moment, Judith pictured her two oldest granddaughters and how much they'd love these little houses. But then she remembered and shook her head no. "That's nice of you to offer, Betty. But I don't think so. Not this year." She started walking toward the front door of the store. "Even if I did, who would ever see them?"

11

After leaving the store with the Christmas village displays, Judith and Betty had browsed through two others on the same side of the street. Judith's mood was improving, at least somewhat. After coming out of the last store, Betty had turned to her and said, "Are you excessively diverted yet, my dear?" She laughed, admitting she and one of her daughters had watched a Jane Austen movie yesterday while the boys watched football.

"I wouldn't say excessively," Judith replied. "Perhaps merely . . . diverted."

"I just love the way they talked back then," Betty said. "They use words we never say anymore, but ones that fit perfectly in the situation."

Judith remembered one of her favorite quotes from *Sense and Sensibility*. She and Betty had watched it last month, for maybe the tenth time. "Remember what Colonel Brandon said in *Sense and Sensibility* when he was worrying about Marianne being so sick? 'Give me an occupation, Miss Dashwood, or I shall run mad.'"

"I do. And see? It fits perfectly. That's what I'm doing here today, with you. You were stuck at home, brooding, going mad, and you needed an occupation. So I've given you one."

"I wasn't exactly going mad."

"In a Jane Austen sort of way, you were," Betty said. "The point is, you needed to get out of the house, get your mind on more pleasant things." Betty looked across the street. They weren't far from the intersection at 4th Avenue. "Like an afternoon caffè breve. I could use a little caffeine, how about you?"

"I think a breve might bring me all the way to excessively diverted," Judith said.

Betty laughed. They watched for traffic, then jaywalked across the street when a safe gap opened up. Their favorite café was only one short block away.

Betty looked at the line once they got inside. "I guess we weren't the only ones who needed to be diverted."

Judith said it would be worth the wait. The line moved fairly quickly, but there were no tables left inside. "Do you want to sit for a spell or keep shopping? There's still a few tables outside. I'm fine either way."

"You fix your breve," Betty said, "and I'll go get us a table." Betty liked her drink just the way it came. "I want to keep shopping, but my feet could use a little rest."

When Judith came out to join her, Betty said, "If you don't mind, I'd like to talk to you about something. I've been thinking about it since we left that store with the little Christmas village display."

Judith sat down. "I don't mind." Of course, she was just being polite. She wouldn't really know if she minded until she heard what Betty had to say.

"It's about you shutting down the idea of buying one of those Christmas houses. I think you said, 'Who would ever see it?'"

"Well, who would?" Judith said. "No one's gonna be there during the holidays but Stan and me. I'm pretty certain he won't care too much about it."

"But I could tell you really liked them. When was the last time you ever bought anything simply because you liked it? Because it made *you* happy?"

Judith thought a moment. Nothing came to mind. She thought some more. Still, nothing.

"See? That's what I'm talking about. Your whole life, for a good long while now, has been centered on your kids and your grandkids. Even on Stan. But as long as I've known you, I've never seen you focus on yourself."

Judith took a sip. "That's been kind of on purpose. Isn't that the definition of being selfish? Focusing on yourself?"

"I'm sure it can be," Betty said. "If that's all someone ever does, or if that's their primary motivation. But that's certainly not your case. If anything, you're on the opposite end of the spectrum. You never focus on yourself. Your whole focus, for years now—really, decades—has been looking after other people. To the point where you feel guilty even thinking about doing something nice for yourself . . . even once."

Judith tried to process this. It did have a ring of truth to it.

"Barney came home from the Bass Pro Shop yesterday with a couple of bags of fishing trinkets. I suppose Stan did too."

"He did."

"Did he apologize for that? 'Cause Barney didn't apologize to me."

"No, he didn't."

"And by the tone of your voice, you weren't expecting an apology either. Neither was I. They didn't feel guilty, and they weren't guilty. Whatever money they spent, they spent on themselves. Now, if they had gone down there and spent so much money we couldn't pay the bills or we ran out of food before the next payday, that would be a totally different thing. But that's never happened, and I don't see it happening anytime soon."

"No," Judith said, "I see your point."

"And we won't even talk about the amount of money they've saved up for that new boat they want to buy. Their dream rig. I don't know what it's up to now, but I know it's several thousand dollars apiece."

"I suppose it is."

"The amount of money's not really the point. The point is they're not feeling guilty about it. Their focus is not on you or me, or the kids, or the grandkids. Of course, they like to talk about all the fun the family will have once they get it. But we both know, and they know too, that's not why they're buying that boat. It makes them happy, and we love them—such as they are—so we're glad they're happy. As long as they don't go crazy, that is."

Betty was right. Stan's fishing hobby had never bothered her that much. She felt like he worked hard, always had, and he'd never been extravagant with his purchases.

"And there's something else," Betty continued. "Not only should you *not* feel any guilt if you *do* want to start collecting those little Christmas houses, you shouldn't worry whether or not anyone else will see them. Even if you're the only one who does . . . if you enjoy them, that matters. Of course, that'll never happen. It'll never be just you. I'll come see it. Maybe I'll even go in on it with you. It could be our hobby, like Stan and Barney's fishing thing."

Judith smiled and took another sip of her breve. Betty was talking crazy, but still she enjoyed hearing her efforts to cheer her up.

Betty set her coffee cup down. "So . . . are we going back?"

"Going back where?"

"To the first store, the one with the Christmas village."

"I don't know."

"What don't you know? Your face lit up when we were in there."

"I'll think about it. I thought they were cute. I did. I'm not sure I'm ready to adopt a full-fledged hobby just yet."

Betty stood. "Okay. Let's walk through a few more stores, and you think about it. But think about this, while you're at it. Hobbies like that are something you do a little each year, not all at once. I know the kids aren't coming home this year, but who knows about next year or the year after that? Anything can happen."

12

Stan arrived home from work shortly after five. It had been a long day working at Home Depot. He was semi-retired and normally only worked four hours a day. They had called him in early to help with the holiday rush. He hadn't been on his feet for ten hours in a row for quite some time, and his legs ached.

He knew Judith wasn't going to be home. They'd spoken briefly on the phone right after Stan had clocked out. She was still shopping downtown with Betty. The plan was for him and Barney to hurry down there to meet the girls for dinner before the Light Up ceremony began at six thirty. He was looking forward to sitting in a restaurant booth, getting some time off his feet. He had decided to skip his shower but wanted to come home and change first, at least clean up a little.

Stan was about ready to head out the door but stopped at the kitchen cabinet where they kept their over-the-counter meds to get some ibuprofen. He grabbed three of them, then walked through the living room and turned on a few lights. It would be dark out by the time they returned.

He stood a moment and stared at the little Christmas tree, then looked down at the three boxes of ornaments on the coffee table. The top box looked like it had been moved a bit and messed with a little, but Judith still hadn't put any ornaments on the tree. And the two containers of decorations were still unopened on the dining room table.

Stan was starting to get a little concerned. He had seen her depressed before but never like this. When he had called her earlier from work, he was tired enough to suggest that she and Betty eat dinner downtown without him. Something told him not to, that he better go ahead and go. As he exited the house and locked the front door, he wondered if Judith's time out with Betty had done her some good.

If she couldn't get into a Christmas mood after spending all that time in downtown Mount Dora during the opening holiday weekend, Stan didn't know if anything could turn her around.

Betty figured they had probably just walked into their final store of the day, considering their husbands were on their way to join them. Judith did seem to be doing a little better, but she still hadn't shown any interest in going back to that first store and starting her Christmas village collection. The store they had just entered was called Crafts & Such. Betty always enjoyed this store.

It looked like it could be one of those stores that sold only Christmas items year-round, judging by the inventory on display. But she'd been in here before. The store changed its stock to feature whatever new season was coming next. After Christmas, it would probably shift to Valentine's Day. One whole section was devoted to handmade Christmas ornaments. Betty pointed them out to Judith and said, "They're nice, but I don't see any shrunken heads or shrieking ghosts." Judith actually laughed.

In the middle of the store, Betty picked up a cute reindeer made mostly from felt wrapped around an empty toilet paper roll. "I never knew there were so many different things people could turn into Christmas decorations."

"I know," Judith said. "Look at these. They're made from popsicle sticks." She pointed at a basket filled with skinny wooden Santa Clauses, snowmen, elves, and reindeer.

"I just passed a woman who works here," Betty said. "I heard her talking to a customer. She said everything in here is handmade, even hand painted."

Judith turned one over. "I wonder where they're made," she said.

They continued to browse for several more minutes. Betty went down another aisle and found a section of craft supplies toward the back of the store. Again, all of them seemed to feature Christmas themes. She also noticed she was the only one in this part of the store. Everyone else browsed through the already-made things in the front half of the store. As she looked at the items more closely, she realized these craft supplies resembled the already-made things up front. Maybe these were the raw materials to make them.

"Are you interested in making things yourself?"

Betty turned. A woman about her same age stood behind her, wearing a name badge that said Doris. "Oh no, I'm terrible at crafts. But my friend over there"—she pointed to Judith, who was still standing in the middle of the store— "she's very talented. You know that big craft fair we have here in Mount Dora every October? I tell her every year she should set up a booth and sell the things she makes."

"We sell a lot of craft supplies," the woman said. "But they're not such big sellers year-round. The already-made crafts are, though. I've been thinking of shutting down this section to use the space for something else. I guess people are just too busy anymore to take the time to make things like this."

"Are you the store owner?" Betty asked.

Doris nodded.

"People are a lot busier now than they used to be," Betty said. "And more women working outside the home than there used to be. You can see it in the grocery store. When I was first married, you only saw one or two racks of already-made dinners in the frozen food section."

"TV dinners, we called them."

Betty smiled. "Salisbury steak, peas, and flaky mashed potatoes, in little tin trays. But look at it now, they devote two whole aisles to premade meals. I still cook most of the time, but my husband and I've tried quite a few of those premade things. Some of them are pretty good."

"It's a different world than when I got married," Doris said. "Like Bob Dylan sang, the times they are a-changin'."

Betty looked down the aisle at Judith, who was holding a snowman made from an upside-down Styrofoam cup and ball. An idea suddenly popped into her mind. "Doris—may I call you Doris?"

"By all means."

"Maybe the reason these do-it-yourself things aren't selling very well isn't just because people are so busy these days. What if it was something else? Something you can fix?"

"Like what?"

"I think it may have more to do with people not knowing how to make things from scratch anymore. People being busy is part of the problem, I'm sure. But what if it's also that they wouldn't know how to turn all these craft items into something fun all by themselves? Without anyone's help?"

"What are you suggesting?" Doris said.

"See the woman I came in with?" She pointed to Judith. Doris nodded.

"I happen to know that every year at Christmas when her kids were younger, they would make Christmas ornaments together, from scratch. She would come up with the ideas, buy all the stuff, then show them how to make it. She's got a whole box of homemade Christmas ornaments at home. I just saw them yesterday. Some of them turned out absolutely hilarious. But it was clear to me they had a blast making them together, and they made some memories she still gets choked up about whenever she tells the story."

"You mean have a craft class here, making ornaments?"

Betty nodded. "A mother-daughter class. They could make Christmas ornaments together. You could have them on Saturday mornings. To get more people in, you could offer the classes for free. Moms would just have to agree to buy the craft supplies from your store."

Doris thought a moment and looked down at all the craft

supplies in front of her. A big smile came over her face. "I think that's a great idea. Do you think your friend would do it? How much would she charge?"

Betty looked at Judith. "I don't know if she'll do it. I just thought of the idea right now, but I can ask her. I wouldn't be surprised if she'd do it as a volunteer."

"Really? You think so?"

"I don't know. If she says yes, are you interested?"

"Definitely," Doris said. "When could she start? Christmas isn't that far away."

13

Judith looked at her watch. They needed to get going. They were supposed to meet their husbands in five minutes at the little park on the corner of 4th Avenue and Alexander Street. She looked over at Betty, who had just waved good-bye to a store worker she had been talking to. Both women were smiling.

"Do you see the time?" Betty said.

They began walking toward the front door. "Yes. We don't want to give the boys a reason to complain if we have to wait in line at the restaurant." Stan hated waiting in line at restaurants. It was second only to his hatred of being stuck in bumper-to-bumper traffic.

"I thought we had reservations."

"We do," Judith said. "But if we're too late, we'll lose them. What were you and that woman talking about?"

"She's the store owner," Betty said as they stepped out onto the sidewalk. "I was just looking at all of the craft supplies. She was telling me how they don't sell very well anymore. She said most people just buy the crafts already finished. I told her how you always made Christmas ornaments from scratch with your kids all those years."

She looked like she had more to say, but she stopped talking as they crossed the street. When they arrived at the park, Barney was there but not Stan. Judith looked around and didn't see him anywhere. She looked at Barney. "Have you seen Stan?"

"Nope. But I just got here a few minutes ago myself."

Judith's cell phone chimed, telling her she had a text. She pulled it out of her purse. It was Stan. "Here he is." She read the message. "He said he's running a few minutes late and will meet us at the restaurant. He's almost there."

"Let's go then," Barney said. "There's a lot more people 'round here than normal. If we miss our reservation, they're likely to give our table away. Then we'd be stuck waiting for who knows how long."

It only took a few minutes to reach the restaurant. They had eaten there before, and Judith liked it. It specialized in Cuban cuisine.

When they got to the front door, Barney said, "I'll go see where things are at." He gave the hostess their names, then came back and said with a tone of significant satisfaction, "We made it. Less than a five-minute wait."

The ladies sat on a small bench in the reception area. Barney stood next to Betty. Judith noticed a little Christmas tree on the counter, with looped red and silver garland tacked underneath. Christmas knickknacks sat along the windowsill.

They did nothing for her.

The front door opened, a little bell rang. It was Stan. He smiled at Judith, then looked at Barney. "We too late? Did we lose our reservation?"

Barney shook his head. "She should be back here any minute to show us to our table."

Stan walked over and stood beside Judith. "So how'd your afternoon go? I don't see any packages. Weren't you guys shopping?"

"Browsing mostly," Judith replied.

"I almost had her talked into something," Betty said. "You know those cute little Christmas villages?"

"I've seen 'em," Stan said.

"She was eyeing some of those lit-up little buildings and those ones with moving parts, like kids ice-skating or skiing down little snowy hills."

Stan looked at Judith. "Were they too expensive?"

Judith shrugged. "I didn't even look at the prices."

"Some of them are, the bigger pieces," Betty said. "But I saw quite a few that were probably a lot less than what you boys spent at Bass Pro Shop."

The boys gave her a look. Judith knew that look. They didn't want this conversation to go any deeper. "You don't have to worry. I'm not planning on starting any fancy collection. I just thought they were interesting to look at. Like something in a museum."

"I wasn't worried," Stan said.

The hostess came up and announced, "If you'll follow me, your table is ready."

The dinner conversation was pleasant enough, but to Stan, Judith seemed pretty distant. Several times during idle moments when everyone else was eating, Stan would catch her staring out the window, her fork stuck in her dish of *ropa vieja*. He thought about asking her what she was thinking about, but he figured he already knew. *What's Suzanne doing right now in Fort Worth? Or Anna in Virginia? Brandon out in Denver? What kind of day are the grandkids having . . . without me, and so far away?* He wished she would snap out of it. There wasn't anything either of them could do to fix it.

Darkness was setting in outside. He looked at his watch.

"I was thinking," Barney said, "we better start wrapping things up in here. They'll be turning the Christmas lights on in a few minutes."

Stan could see the people on the sidewalks all moving in the same direction, heading to Donnelly Park. Looking at Judith's plate, he said, "You want to get a container for that?"

She looked down. Her food, barely touched. "Yes, that would be nice."

He signaled for the waitress, and she brought the check. He asked for a container; they only needed one.

"Looks like a lot more people in town than last year," Betty said.

"A lot of the bigger Florida cities don't have the kind of small-town Christmas traditions we have around here. I think folks that moved down from up north kind of miss that, and word is catching on."

After paying their bill and leaving a tip, they made their way out to the sidewalk to join everyone else heading for the Light Up ceremony.

When they reached the park, as expected, a crowd had already gathered to watch the Christmas-themed entertainment and listen to the music. The program had begun forty-five minutes ago. That was the time they used to arrive when the kids were here. Betty had suggested they skip the first part and eat instead, thinking it would minimize the memories of years past.

Maybe it helped some, but not much. As soon as they arrived, Judith kept noticing one family after another sitting together on chairs and blankets. Grandparents sitting near their married children, holding their fidgety grandchildren, faces all turned to take in the live show.

"I see a clear spot over there," Barney said. He led the way.

The size of the crowd and the chill in the air drew them closer than they would normally stand. It was almost completely dark now, just a thin rim of burnt-orange light remaining in the western sky.

A few minutes more and the final singer of the night ended her last Christmas carol. The crowd applauded. They watched as the mayor stepped forward and said a few appropriate holiday words. Then it was time to officially "flip the switch."

Judith's eyes fixed on the surrounding trees in the park. Suddenly, the entire downtown area lit up with the glow of two million sparkling Christmas lights and several thousand cheers and ooh-ahs. Then more applause.

"So beautiful," Betty said.

"It never gets old," Barney said.

"Now, aren't you glad you came?" Stan asked Judith.

"It really is nice," she said. And she felt that way right up until she saw a young woman standing a few yards in front of her, rocking a stroller. From behind, she looked just like Suzanne. The same hair color, the same hairstyle. Wearing a pink jacket similar to one she had bought Suzanne. The toddler in the stroller, a little girl with curly blonde hair, just about the same age as her granddaughter, Brianna.

The resemblance was so keen that for a moment Judith could imagine it really was Suzanne and Brianna. So close she could reach out and touch them. The young woman turned to look at the lights down the street, instantly ending the fantasy.

14

It was Sunday. Judith had made it through church okay.

She walked out into the parking lot, Stan by her side. She was pretty sure when she had shaken the pastor's hand by the front door—judging by his smile—he wouldn't have been too happy to hear her describe her condition as "made it through." After all the work he had likely put into that sermon, he probably would have hoped to lift her spirits to someplace higher than just "okay."

But he had accomplished a great deal, considering that when she had woken up this morning, she had no desire to go to church and seriously considered staying home.

"Want to go out and grab a bite to eat?" Stan asked when they reached the car. "I'm buying."

She smiled. "We could. I've got those bass you caught Friday morning ready to cook. I don't mind going home and doing that."

"Maybe we'll have those later on for supper. I'm kind of ready to eat now."

She actually was a little hungry today, and she sure didn't mind putting off work a little longer. "I'll go wherever you drive."

"How about we go over to that Chinese buffet? I'm kind of in the mood for Chinese."

"Sounds good."

He clicked the button on the keychain, the car doors unlocked, and they got in. As he pulled out of the parking lot, he said, "Since we just came out of church, I've got a confession to make."

"Oh?"

"I've got an ulterior motive for taking you out just now. I'm kind of hoping that between the inspiration of church and not having to make dinner, you might have enough energy to do some Christmas decorating at the house this afternoon. We don't have to do it all up like we've done in years past. I know that would be a bridge too far. But what do you think? You want to try?"

She really didn't, but it sounded like he was offering to help her. He'd never helped her decorate before. "The way you're talking, it almost sounds like you're doing it with me."

"I am. So, what do you think?"

"Maybe. We'll see."

They got home from the Chinese buffet about an hour later. Judith put some coffee on, and they both changed into more relaxing clothes. She actually felt a little stuffed, even though she had eaten only one plate of food. That old saying that if you eat Chinese you'll be hungry an hour later didn't seem to apply to buffet food.

She walked into the kitchen to find Stan cutting himself a slice of pumpkin pie. She couldn't believe it. He had gone back for seconds at the buffet. "I couldn't even think about eating pie right now."

"I love Chinese but not their desserts. So, I left a little room. How long before that coffee is ready?"

"I think it's ready now," she said. "Can you get out two mugs?" She fixed her coffee and started walking toward the Florida room. She heard Stan's footsteps behind her.

"Where are you going?"

She stopped and turned. "What do you mean, where am I going? In here, to drink my coffee."

"I thought we were going to do some decorating together."

He was serious. "Don't you want to eat your pie first?"

"That'll take me two minutes."

"Let me get this straight . . . you're really planning on helping?"

"Well, yeah. That's what together means. You might have to help me some, to know where things go. It's not like I've got too much practice."

"Not too much, eh?"

"Okay, I've got no practice. You and the kids used to do all this while Barney and I went fishing."

She wished he hadn't reminded her about that.

"So . . . are you gonna stay out here and help me, or do I have to do this all by myself?"

That was a sight she'd like to see. "I guess I could help some. Can I finish my coffee first?"

"Sure. I just figured if you went in the Florida room, I'd lose you for good."

They sat where they always did in the living room. He wasn't kidding about finishing his pie in two minutes. Her eyes moved back and forth between the stack of containers on the dining room table and the three boxes of ornaments on the coffee table in front of her. Normally, she would set out all the decorations around the house then work on the tree. Not that it mattered now.

"Where do you want to start?" Stan said.

"I was just thinking about that. Do you want to do one and I'll do the other? Maybe you should start on the tree since you don't know where any of the decorations go."

He walked his empty pie plate out to the kitchen counter, then came back and stood in front of the boxes of ornaments. "I was thinking we were going to do this together. It shouldn't take too long, right? We don't have to put everything up if you don't want." He opened the flap of the box on top. "Which one is this?" He leaned the box forward and read his own writing. "The ugly ornaments. I remember these."

"Could we not start with them?" She stood and walked toward the dining room table. "Let's start with the house decorations. That's the order I'm used to. We'll set these out, then work on the tree."

"Sounds good."

He said this with an uncharacteristic amount of enthusiasm. She pulled the lid off the first container.

"Snowmen," he said as he got closer. "Where do they go?"

She looked down and began to sort through them with her fingers. Must be twenty of them in here, all different shapes and sizes. Each one occupied a specific place in the house, and she knew exactly where they belonged. "Tell you what, since we're breaking all our traditions this year, just put them up wherever it suits you. Just remember—" Then she stopped. She was just about to tell Stan to put any made of ceramic on the higher shelves, out of the reach of their grandkids' little fingers. But that didn't matter now. None of her grandchildren would be here reaching for things they shouldn't touch. "Just make sure they're not too close to the edge. Since we leave the windows open most of December, the door tends to slam."

"I can do that." He held out his hands. "Fill 'em up with snowmen."

So she did, then picked up two handfuls herself and joined in. Try as she might to break tradition, she wound up placing every single snowman in its previously assigned place. It took about ten minutes. Then they worked through the rest of the container, laying out the angels, then the reindeer and elves.

As she got ready to open the lid on the second container, Stan set the small handful of Christmas elves he'd been holding in an upholstered chair and came over. "What are you doing?" she asked.

"Nothing. I just want to see what's in the next one."

"You have something against elves?"

"No." He didn't say anything more, and he didn't go back to finish with the elves. He just stood there wearing an odd smile. "Well, aren't you going to open it?"

She turned around and took off the lid. At first, she didn't see anything unusual. Just an assortment of familiar-looking Christmas decorations. She looked at him over her shoulder. He was staring into the container at a certain spot. Her eyes traced the direction until she was looking at the same place. That's when she noticed it. A plastic store bag wrapped tightly around a white box. It was the only unfamiliar thing in the container. Lifting it out, she said, "What did you do?"

"Just open it."

As soon as she saw the bag unfurled, she guessed what it was. Lifting the box out confirmed it. "You didn't have to do that." It was a little ceramic house from the Dickens Christmas village she had been looking at with Betty yesterday.

"I know I didn't," he said. "I wanted to do something to cheer you up. Just think of it as an early Christmas present."

She took it carefully out of the box, spun it around slowly in her hands, then set it on the table. It was just as cute as she remembered from the store. She turned around and gave Stan a hug, and he hugged her back. "That was a sweet thing to do." She couldn't remember the last time he'd bought her something as a surprise. She squeezed him a little tighter before letting go.

"Now you can start that collection."

She didn't have the heart to tell him she really was serious about not doing that. Instead, she said nothing and walked the little house to a safe spot on the mantel above the fireplace.

For the next fifteen minutes, they continued to make their way through the other decorations. At one point, Judith stopped to get her cell phone to sneak in a few pics of Stan spending all kinds of time getting the nativity scene just right. She wasn't sure he'd ever even looked at it before now. Anna and Suzanne had to see this.

When they'd finished the second container, Stan was about to open the third, but she said, "I think we've done enough decorating, don't you?"

He stood, scratched his chin, and surveyed the scene. "Yeah, I guess we have. Let's work on the tree."

He walked to the coffee table; she followed behind. The house definitely looked more Christmassy, but it still hadn't impacted her inside. It was pleasant but carried no more weight than the decorations downtown.

Stan opened the ugly ornaments box and pulled out the top three ornaments, the ones wrapped in green paper, the kids' favorites, and set them on the coffee table. He picked up the first one, the biggest one—Anna's blue pinecone—and began to unwrap it.

Without thinking, she walked up, stopped him, and gently took it out of his hand. She wrapped it back up, set it carefully in the box. Then picked up the other two ornaments, put them in the box, and closed the flaps.

"What's the matter? Did I do something wrong?"

"I don't think I can do this."

"Do what? Decorate the tree?"

She nodded.

"We just gonna leave it like that? Just the lights, no ornaments?"

"No, I guess not. But I don't want to put up these ornaments, the ones the kids made. Especially those three, the ones wrapped in green. Those were their favorites. I don't think I could bear to look at them every day until Christmas."

"Are you okay with using the other two boxes then?"

"I guess we could do that. Just not ones from this box."

"What do you want me to do with it?"

"I don't know. Maybe put it back in the attic. It makes me too sad to look at it."

15

The next morning around nine thirty, Judith walked into the living room wearing her sneakers, shorts, and a light sweatshirt. She was about to meet Betty in the driveway for a walk. Betty worked part-time at Hobby Lobby but didn't go in till after lunch today. She'd called about thirty minutes ago, more or less telling Judith it was far too nice a morning to waste it by staying indoors. They should take a walk, which Betty was certain would do Judith a world of good.

Besides, she'd said, she had something she wanted to talk to Judith about, and a walk would give her the perfect opportunity.

Judith wished Betty had left that last part out of the conversation, because now she kept trying to figure out what it could be. She stepped on the throw rug in the middle of the room and began a few stretching exercises. As she did, she noticed the little Christmas village house Stan had surprised her with yesterday sitting on the fireplace mantel. She still couldn't believe Stan had done that.

She finished her exercises, walked over, and picked it up. Actually, it wasn't the one she'd had her eye on at the store. It was the piece behind it. But that didn't matter. It was the thought, and still, it was very cute. She wished it could have served the purpose he'd intended. It had made her smile several times yesterday and made her feel a little more loved than usual. But she could tell Stan had hoped it would set her firmly on a path out of this depression she'd fallen into. She wished it had.

Her cell phone chimed, signaling a text. It was Betty, saying she was out in the driveway. Judith put the little house back in its place, shoved her cell phone in her pocket, and headed out the front door.

"This weather is perfect," Betty said.

It really was. Maybe the fresh air would do her some good. They had taken walks so many times before, neither one needed to lead the way.

"I heard you finally decorated the house yesterday," Betty said.

"How did you hear that? Did Stan call you?"

"Let's just say . . . he and I talked."

Judith thought a minute. "So, it was your idea. What Stan did. The Christmas house, helping me decorate."

"Okay, it was. But as soon as I suggested it, he actually liked the idea. So, did he wind up doing both things?"

They reached the corner and turned right. "Yes, he did," Judith said. She replayed how Stan had pulled off the surprise.

"That sounds almost romantic," Betty said. "So, did he help you decorate the tree too?"

"Yes, he did."

Betty looked at Judith. "But you don't seem like it did the trick. You still seem kind of down."

Judith sighed. "I know. I kind of still am. I don't want to be. I'm not trying to be. I really appreciate what you both did, conspiring to buy me that present yesterday. And it was nice decorating the house with Stan. That's the first time we've done that since the kids were born."

"But it didn't fix what's broken," Betty said.

Judith shook her head no. "I wish it had."

They walked past a few houses in silence.

Then Betty said, "Don't be too hard on yourself. We don't have switches like the guys do."

"What do you mean?"

"Switches for our emotions. We can't just turn them off and on whenever we want. I'm always surprised by how quickly Barney can just shut down his feelings. Things upset him, but only for a little while. Then he just decides to stop letting them. Stop thinking about it, stop feeling anything about it. And he just moves on. Sometimes I hate how easily he does it."

"Stan is kind of like that too."

"The thing with Barney is, sometimes he flips that switch off way before I want him to. Like after he's done something hurtful or insensitive. I want him to feel bad about it longer than he usually does. Long enough to where he starts to care and maybe think twice about doing the same thing again. He'll say he's sorry, I can tell he probably is, but it feels too fast. Then he flips that switch, and he's all done. Case closed."

Judith smiled. She could relate to that. "Well, I can tell Stan is at least trying this time. He didn't say it, but I could tell last night he would've liked it if I could have found that switch. He was disappointed his efforts hadn't yielded better results."

They reached a four-way stop sign and waited for a lone car to pass, then crossed the street. The next block was nice and shady.

"I'm sure you'll come out of this when you're ready," Betty said. "I was thinking of that proverb, the one that says, 'Hope deferred makes the heart sick.' I think that's what's happening here."

Judith knew the proverb and understood the implication. Disappointment, and even downright sadness, were normal when something you hoped for didn't happen. "But doesn't the next part say, 'But a desire fulfilled is a tree of life'? Makes me feel kind of stuck. There's no way what I desire can be fulfilled. Not this year. So, no tree of life for me."

Betty thought a moment. "Guess my Bible verse kind of backfired. I was hoping it would make you feel a little better, knowing what you're going through is normal."

"I'm sorry. It does make me feel a little better. Just taking this walk with you helps some. What Stan did yesterday helps. But it's just . . ."

"It's just *what*? You can say it, whatever it is."

They walked a few moments more. She wasn't sure she should say it out loud or if Betty would understand, could understand.

"C'mon, Judith. What are you thinking?"

"I know this is probably just my depression talking, but I've been trying to figure out what's bugging me, what's keeping me stuck in this hole. And I think . . ." Still, she hesitated to say it.

"What? What is it?"

"It's kind of what that proverb you quoted is saying. I'm struggling because I didn't expect that having my kids and pouring my heart and soul into them all these years, sacrificing all of my hopes and dreams so that they could reach theirs, would end up with me having nothing to show for it in the end. That one by one, in just a few short years, they wouldn't just leave the nest but fly so far away I'd never see them again. Even at Christmas." Tears filled her eyes. "And I know I just said a whole bunch of things that are over the top, but that's exactly how I feel."

She stopped walking and wiped her eyes on her sleeve.

Betty stopped too, leaned over, and gave her a hug. After a few moments, she said, "Yeah, I guess you're gonna need a bit more than a ceramic Christmas house to pull out of this one."

16

Do you want to turn back?" Betty asked.

"No," Judith said, "we've only gone a couple of blocks."

"I know, but maybe this is the kind of conversation we should have in your Florida room over coffee. Or maybe since it's so nice out, in those antique Adirondacks you have parked underneath that big oak tree."

Judith thought a moment. "No, let's just keep walking. If I lose it again, we can turn around." They started walking again. Neither one said anything until they reached the next stop sign.

"I think this expectation thing with your kids is pretty widespread," Betty said. "I mean, feeling disappointed that things haven't gone the way you planned. I know lots of parents our age feel that way."

Judith didn't know if she should say the other thing she was thinking. Betty was only trying to help.

"I know that look," Betty said.

What kind of look was she giving? Judith wasn't even aware her expression had changed. "What are you talking about?"

"You think my expectations have all been met, with my kids, I mean. Because they're all still living in town, and they were all there at the house on Thursday. And you're wondering how can I really understand what you're going through since our situations are so different."

Betty had nailed it. "I still appreciate you being here, though," Judith said. "Helping me talk this out. I know it's always better to talk things out when you're hurting rather than to bottle them up inside."

"That's why we live ten years longer than men," Betty said. "But I wasn't just trying to comfort you by saying that. I think I understand your frustration a little more than you might imagine."

They stepped out of the shady area and were now walking in the sun again. The warmth on her face felt nice. "Okay, I'm listening."

"It's true, our kids are still living nearby. And I'm not going to lie, it's especially nice at holidays and birthdays. But things with our three kids aren't exactly where we'd like them to be either. Especially with Ethan." Ethan was their youngest, the only one still living at home. "It's got Barney pretty frustrated. I don't know if he's ever mentioned anything to Stan."

"If so, Stan hasn't said."

Betty smiled, shook her head. "It's crazy how men are.

You'd think as long as he and Stan have been friends, he'd open up about it. With me, he goes back and forth between feeling hurt by Ethan and getting angry. Happened again at Thanksgiving."

"Really?" Judith said. "How come you and I have never talked about it?"

"Because it's not something that eats at me the way it does him. I guess I have my expectations set lower than Barney does. I see Ethan just being pretty much the way boys his age are. Especially nowadays."

"What does Ethan do that bugs Barney?"

"He's hardly ever home, for one thing. Between work and hanging out with his friends, we barely see him. He's hardly even home for dinner, except maybe twice a week."

"Is he hanging out with the wrong kind of friends?" Judith said. "Is he getting in any trouble, coming home drunk? Things like that?"

"Not really. He stays out way too late. We both don't like that. But his friends are all the kids who grew up in church together. Now they're all young adults, most in their early twenties. Barney says that they don't act like adults, at least not the way we acted when we were their age. They hang out together at each other's places. Sometimes they play Xbox tournaments well into the night or watch movies. They don't seem all that focused on getting good jobs or settling down. But I don't think those are the biggest things that bug Barney."

Judith knew those things would've bugged Stan, had Brandon gone that way. But Brandon had been pretty serious-minded about college right out of high school. "So, what bothers Barney the most?"

"It's that same unmet expectations thing you and I were

talking about. That 'hope deferred makes the heart sick' thing. See, Barney and his dad were never close. He always wished they were, but his father was a workaholic. The kind of father more focused on his career than on spending time with his kids. His dad saw his primary job as putting a roof over their heads and keeping food on the table. He wasn't into having a relationship with Barney or his siblings. Barney said he never showed up to any of his Little League games. They hardly did anything together. He can't remember ever having a single meaningful talk with his dad his whole life."

Judith's memories of her father were eerily similar. "I think a lot of men in that era were like that."

"You're probably right," Betty said. "But my dad wasn't one of them. He was a great dad growing up. I remember when I was pregnant with our first, Barney said he was gonna fix that with our kids. Be more like my dad than his. And he was. He turned down all kinds of promotions over the years, made sure he could be there for the kids, for everything. Never missed a birthday, never missed a holiday or a ballet recital for the girls. He didn't just attend Ethan's ball games, he was his coach. And he took him with him whenever he went out, tried to take an interest in everything going on in Ethan's life."

Judith could see where this was going. "Barney thought spending all that time with Ethan growing up would guarantee they'd have a close father-son friendship when Ethan got older."

Betty nodded. "You got it. But that's not what happened." After the next intersection, the road started going downhill. It caused their pace to pick up a little steam. Betty continued. "I remember Barney and I having a talk a few years ago about how his friendship with Ethan might affect his relationship with Stan. Barney was concerned it might be a little awkward if he started including Ethan in the times he hung out with Stan."

Judith didn't recall that ever being a problem. Now she understood why.

"Of course," Betty said, "that's not where things ended up. Right about the time Ethan graduated from high school, we could feel him starting to pull away. He was spending more and more time with his friends and less and less time with us. Their friendship dried up completely. I was kind of expecting it. It hurt some, but it really got to Barney. He felt like after all that time he'd invested in the relationship, he would mean a little more to Ethan than he did. And Ethan would want to be with him more than with his friends."

"But that didn't happen," Judith said.

"No, it didn't. Not only did Barney's friendship expectation fall flat, Ethan doesn't even ask him for advice, even in things Barney could help him with. And sure, Ethan was there for Thanksgiving, for the dinner and dessert. But he was gone an hour later and didn't come home until we were ready for bed."

Judith felt bad for Barney. She had no idea he was going through this.

"Barney reminded me one time of that seventies song 'Cat's in the Cradle' by Harry Chapin. You remember it?"

Judith involuntarily started humming the tune.

"That's it," Betty said. "Remember how it goes? The dad's so busy he misses everything going on while his son is growing up."

Judith nodded. "And he always promises it will be different later."

Betty finished with the last line and said, "But that's not what happens, because they never get together. The dad's always too busy. Barney said when that song came out, it made him cry, because it was exactly what was going on between him and his dad. So, he was determined not to let that happen with Ethan." Betty sighed. "Barney had tears in his eyes Thanksgiving night before we went to bed. He'd heard that song on the car radio, and now, just like the song, the son is avoiding his dad and doesn't have any time for him. Barney said it wasn't fair. That's not how it was supposed to turn out, because he did all those things with Ethan his dad never did with him. But still, it didn't matter. Ethan pulled away, and Barney feels like they're no closer than he was with his dad."

They reached the bottom of the hill, crossed the street, and started walking back in the other direction. "I'm so glad Barney and Stan have stayed good friends," Betty said. "I'm not sure there'd be any living with Barney otherwise."

"Do you think I should mention any of this to Stan? Maybe he could figure out a tactful way to get Barney to open up to him."

"I suppose it wouldn't hurt. But I wouldn't try too hard. I don't think Barney's hiding it from him. I think by the time they get together after Barney's had one of these Ethan disappointments, he's already tucked any negative emotions into one of his many compartments."

It was hard to believe how differently men processed things. Judith's legs felt the tension of walking uphill, but her mind felt a little more at ease. It was somehow comforting to know that Betty could relate to her struggle, at least in part.

17

After their walk brought them back around to Judith's house, she invited Betty in.

"I better not," Betty said. "I need to get home and get cleaned up for work. But if you don't mind, I'd like to keep you for another minute or two. We spent so much time talking about other things, I never got around to the thing I really wanted to ask you about this morning."

Judith had forgotten all about that. "Okay."

"Let's talk in the shade," Betty said. "Wish it was a little cooler out, to make it feel more Christmassy."

They moved off the driveway into the side yard. "So what's this all about?"

"It's not a big thing," Betty said. "It's just an idea. It kind of goes along with what we've been talking about on our walk."

"About my depression?"

"Yeah. I've thought of something I think might help. The idea came to me when we were visiting that last store on Saturday, the craft store."

"When you were talking with the owner?"

"Yes. She was saying she might have to close down that whole make-it-yourself section in the back of the store. Nobody has time to make crafts anymore. They all just want to buy things already made."

"And you don't think that's true?" Judith said.

"I think it's partly true. A lot more moms are working full-time now, but I don't think that's the only reason. Remember last summer at church when I helped out at that young moms workshop?"

Judith nodded. "Suzanne went to it. I remember she liked it a lot."

"I remember thinking as I listened that a lot of what they were teaching were the kinds of things moms used to teach their daughters themselves, day by day as they grew up. We would never have thought about going to a class to learn them. But these young mothers were eating it up, asking all kinds of questions. They really wanted to learn these things. It made me realize one of the casualties of modern life is this communication breakdown. The mentoring that moms used to do with their daughters that women our age take for granted."

Judith could kind of see this, although she'd worked hard to teach the basics, even more than the basics, to Anna and Suzanne as they grew up. "So what does this have to do with the craft store we visited Saturday, or with me?"

"I think the same thing's going on with this craft store,"

Betty said. "Moms don't make things anymore with their kids, because no one's ever taught them how. But I think most people will try something new if there's someone there willing to lead them through it, step-by-step."

"And what do you think I should do about this?"

"Have a class," Betty said. "That's what I was talking to the owner about Saturday. I told her how you taught your kids to make ornaments from scratch every year throughout their childhood. You know all those handmade ornaments you were looking at in the store? Well, she has everything you need to make them right there."

"So you want me to teach a class on making homemade ornaments?"

"On Saturday mornings, right there at the store."

"Betty . . . you've *seen* my ornaments."

Betty smiled. "Doesn't matter. The owner loved the idea. She asked me to ask you if you'd consider it. I told her you might even volunteer. There's just a few Saturdays left before Christmas. But I'm sure she'd consider paying you something to do it. If you say yes, she'll talk it up with her customers and put posters by the front door and the cash register. The class would be free. The moms would just have to agree to buy the supplies for the ornaments there at the store, in that make-it-yourself section."

"So I'd be picking out ornaments to make from the already-made stuff in the store?"

"Either that, or you could come up with something totally original. You'd just have to use craft supplies they have available in the store." Betty stood there a moment in silence. "So, what do you think? Is that something you might like to do?"

"I don't know." A part of her was certainly interested. She

kind of wished Betty hadn't talked to the owner about her teaching the class. She had no idea what she might charge. And it really would only be a handful of Saturdays. *If* she decided to do it. "How much time do I have before she needs an answer?"

"We didn't discuss that," Betty said. "But I think it would be nice if you could tell her in a day or two, especially if you're gonna do it, so she could start promoting it in the store."

Judith didn't reply. She really wasn't sure what to do.

"Well," Betty said, "I think it would be a great idea. Not just for the craft store but even more so for you. It might help you get your mind off of these negative things you can't do anything about. Besides, you really are good at this craft thing."

"I don't know about that," Judith said. "Stan calls them the ugly ornaments for a reason."

Betty laughed. "But your ideas weren't ugly. Besides, how they turn out isn't the point. It's all the fun the moms and kids have making them, and all the memories they'll make. And I think you might even wind up making some nice memories of your own."

18

A few minutes before noon, Stan stepped outside of the Home Depot and headed for his car, which he'd parked in the far end of the parking lot under a cluster of shade trees. He wondered if a cold front might be moving in, because it was actually cooler now than it had been when he'd pulled in this morning. Stan was on his lunch break. Normally he'd be heading home after four hours, but last night they called and asked if he could work eight today. An unusual number of returns had come in over the weekend.

This wasn't exactly how he wanted to use his one extended break for the day. He pulled out his cell phone as he neared the car. He clicked the button on his keychain, and the doors unlocked. Maybe he would just call them here, sitting in the car. He got in and rolled the front seat windows down, letting a nice breeze blow through. What were the chances he'd reach all three of them the first time he tried?

Calling the kids was more Judith's thing. He was always amazed at how long she could talk with them on the phone and the things she'd come up with to talk about. Of course, he'd eventually get on for a few minutes. Talking with Brandon was the easiest. Brandon would want to brag about something he'd accomplished at work, and he didn't mind listening to a few of Stan's latest fish stories.

But this time, it was all on him. He'd be initiating the calls, and the subject wasn't a pleasant one. In fact, he'd be doing something he didn't really believe in: motivating his kids by guilt. Trying to, anyway. He decided to start with Anna first, since she was the oldest.

The phone rang a few times. "Hey, Dad, is everything all right?"

"'Course everything is all right. Why wouldn't it be?"

"You never call me," Anna said.

She had a point. "Well, everything's fine. Well, not fine. But nothing's wrong. Well, something is wrong, just not serious." Then again, it was kind of serious.

"Dad, what are you talking about?"

"It's your mom."

"What's wrong with Mom?"

"You talked with her on Thanksgiving, couldn't you tell?"

There was a pause. "I guess not. I don't recall us talking about anything being wrong."

"She was probably doing a good job of covering it up then."

"Covering up what?"

"Can't you guess?" he asked.

Another pause. "Do I have to? Can't you just tell me? Did I do something wrong? Did I say something that offended her?"

"You didn't do anything wrong, though you did say something that . . . well, I guess it isn't right to say you offended her. More like disappointed her. But in kind of a big way."

"I disappointed her?" A few moments of silence. "You mean about Christmas, about not making it home for Christmas?"

"Bingo."

"I guess that really upset her, huh?"

"Kinda did."

"She didn't let on that it bothered her."

"Well, you know your mom. She's not going to show something like that over the phone. She wouldn't want to make you upset."

"But I guess it must have, quite a lot. Or you wouldn't be calling me."

"She wouldn't even decorate the house or the Christmas tree on Friday."

"She wouldn't?"

"I got the boxes down from the attic, went off fishing with Barney like I always do, came home to find them sitting right where I'd left them. And she didn't touch them all day Saturday, either. I'm pretty sure she would've ignored them on Sunday, except I offered to help her put them up."

"*You* decorated the house?"

"And the tree." Stan thought about telling Anna about the little Christmas house he'd bought her mother but decided against it.

"That's so sad," Anna said.

"What? Me decorating?"

"No, that Mom's doing so badly. I hate to think of her being so down."

"She's as down as I've ever seen her, Anna. Maybe more. She heard the same thing about not coming home for Christmas from your brother and sister when she called them."

"Neither one of them is coming home for Christmas?"

"Nope. They both said they can't afford it."

"So no family home for Thanksgiving or Christmas," Anna said.

"Nope. Except me. But no kids, and no grandkids either." A pause. Stan waited a moment, wondered what he should say next.

"Poor Mom."

That was good. That was a start.

"Did decorating the house and the tree help her mood any?"

"Not even a little," Stan said. "In fact, she asked me to put away the ugly ornaments."

"They're cute, Dad. Not ugly."

"Well, you know the ones I mean. She had me put them back up in the attic. Said she couldn't bear to look at them."

"Did she say it like she was mad or like she was hurt?"

"She's not mad. She knows you love to come home for the holidays. And you would if you could. Which is why I'm calling, I guess. To make sure there's no way you can come home. Is that a definite impossibility?" He looked at his watch to make sure he was doing okay on the time.

"I'm afraid so," she said. "Bruce found out he isn't getting his Christmas bonus this year. That's what we've been using to come home with every year. They told the employees before the Thanksgiving holiday so they wouldn't make any plans that depended on it."

Stan sighed. That pretty much seemed like a closed door.

"I'm sorry to hear that. But don't worry about it. I still haven't called your brother and sister. Maybe one of them will be able to come. I know you would if you could."

"I really would, Dad. Money's the only reason. Otherwise, we'd be there for sure."

19

After his conversation with Anna, Stan had called his other two children but got voice mail for both. He took a few minutes to eat his tuna-fish sandwich. Every now and then, he checked his watch to make sure of the time.

Just as he popped the last bite into his mouth, his phone rang. It was Brandon. He chewed fast but answered before he'd finished.

"Hey, Dad. Got your message. What's up? Is everything okay?"

"Everything's fine. Didn't I say that on my voice message, that this wasn't an emergency?"

"You did. But you also didn't say what this is about, and you never call me, so I figured something must be up."

That was true. Something was up. "Appreciate you calling

me back so quick. I know you're a busy man these days, so I'll keep this short." He figured the straight approach would work best for Brandon. "It's about your mom. She's not doing too well. Actually, she's been more depressed the last few days than I've ever seen her."

"She has? Do you know why?"

"Oh yeah. She's not hiding the reason."

"I guess it has something to do with me then."

"Not just you. Your sisters too."

"Did we do something wrong?"

"No, not wrong. How about you stop asking me questions, and I'll tell you what it is."

"Okay. Go ahead."

"You know this past Thursday was the first Thanksgiving that none of you kids were here for the holiday."

"I know. I felt bad when I found out. We had a pretty full group out here. Several of our friends from church are in the same boat. Came out here for work, and now we live too far away to get home for the holidays. So we ate together. Plenty of people, plenty of food, plenty of noise. But it wasn't the same."

He and Judith had plenty of food, but that was about it. The silence at the table had been almost unbearable. Of course, he didn't want to say that. "I'm glad you missed being here. We sure missed you. Your mom really struggled. That's really why I'm calling. Turns out, after talking with your sisters, she found out none of you can make it home for Christmas. I think that's what really set her off. No family at Thanksgiving and now none at Christmas. She's pretty much been in a pit ever since."

Brandon said nothing for a few moments. So Stan continued.

"A moment ago, you said you ate Thanksgiving with some friends who live too far away to get home for the holidays. Is that the only thing keeping you?"

"I guess," Brandon said. "We don't have the money to fly, and with gas prices, hotel bills, and eating out all those days, driving costs almost as much as flying. Besides that, it's a three-day drive there and a three-day drive home. And that's if we gun it, which is hard to do driving with kids. I only get a week off this Christmas, so we'd spend all of the time traveling. None of that matters anyway. I don't have enough money to afford either option. The employee part of our health-care plan just went through the roof. I had to cut out our vacation budget, our clothing budget, and our Christmas fund by half just to close the gap."

Brandon sounded worse off than Anna did. "I'm sorry things have gotten so tight for you guys."

"Me too."

"Well, I'll talk to Mom. Maybe we can put a few dollars extra in the Christmas card we send for the kids' presents."

"You don't have to do that, Dad. That's not why I brought that up."

"I know, I know. And I know you guys would come home if you could."

"We definitely would, Dad. I feel bad for making Mom so sad."

"I'm sure she'll be fine. We'll just have to learn to adjust. Life doesn't always turn out like you planned."

"No, it doesn't," Brandon said. "Maybe one thing we could do is talk to each other using Skype or FaceTime. That way we can at least see each other while we're talking."

Neither Stan nor Judith were very tech savvy. "You'd have to help us set that up. Is it very complicated?"

"Not really. I'll email you some step-by-step instructions. Maybe we can do a few practice runs before Christmas."

"I'm sure willing to try it." At least this was something new and different he could share with Judith. Although Stan doubted it would bring her out of this slump she was in.

Stan got the car all locked up and was just about to head back into work when his phone rang again. It was Suzanne. He hadn't even left the shade of the trees yet. He looked at his watch. Eight minutes till he had to clock back in. He'd better keep walking. "Hey, Suzanne. Thanks for calling me back."

"No problem. Your message said it wasn't an emergency, but you never call so I knew I should call back right away. What's going on?"

"I can't talk too long. I'm just finishing my lunch break. Gotta clock back in to work."

"I thought you were just part-time now."

"I am, usually. It's just the holidays making things a little busier than usual."

"Is everything okay?"

Stan spent the next few minutes covering the same ground with Suzanne that he had with Brandon and Anna. Suzanne and her mother were the closest of the three kids. That showed in her reaction. She actually started to cry when Stan mentioned that none of the kids were going to make it home for Christmas, and how sad and depressed Judith had been the last several days.

"I wish there was something I could do," she said. "I didn't say anything to Mom on Thanksgiving, but I was pretty depressed myself. Our table seemed empty Thursday. I made everything Mom makes, just the way she taught me. Even set the table the same way she did. But it didn't do any good."

"I don't know how we're going to get through Christmastime, if your mom's doing this poorly at Thanksgiving," Stan said. "There's absolutely no way you and Todd could make it home this year?"

"Oh Dad, I wish we could. We used up all our savings on this move. Todd and I were talking last night. We're probably going to have to get used toys for Brianna this year. That's how tight things are."

Stan was about to ask if he could put some money toward flying her home for Christmas. Just her. But he instantly realized how stupid that was. A mom leaving her child and husband at Christmas to visit her mother. It was an insane idea. "Well, I thought I'd call and ask, just in case there was a chance. But I guess it's not meant to be, not this year. Brandon suggested we could all use Skype so we can at least see each other while we talk. Ever use that?"

"I have. Anna and I have talked a few times with it."

"You think that's something your mom and I can manage?"

"I'm sure you could. We'd just have to show you a few things."

Stan sighed. "I guess that's something, anyway."

20

Suzanne remained bummed out pretty much all afternoon, ever since the phone call from her dad. She hated thinking about her mom being so down. The holidays were Mom's favorite time of the year. Always had been. It wasn't just the decorations and the music and all the holiday food. It was the extra family time, reliving all the fond memories together and making new ones. And Mom had always made the holidays so much fun, ever since they were kids.

When they had spoken on the phone Thanksgiving Day, Suzanne hadn't detected any sadness in her mom's voice. But she should have. She should've realized how hard it would be for her to suddenly have all of that taken away.

Todd had called about a half hour ago saying he was stuck in traffic, as usual. She should go ahead and eat dinner. When he called, he was already thirty minutes later than normal. But what was normal anymore? He was supposed to get off at five every day and be home by five thirty. She could count the times on one hand that had actually happened. It wasn't his fault. It was the new job, the way they did things. And big-city traffic.

Growing up in Mount Dora, she had thought traffic in Orlando was bad. But the Dallas/Fort Worth area was over three times the size of Orlando. It felt like five times the traffic. Even out here in the suburbs, Suzanne would sometimes feel exhausted by the time she got home from an afternoon of running errands.

There were just so . . . many . . . people.

She glanced at the digital clock on the stove. Unless Todd ran into more surprises, he should be pulling up in the driveway any minute. Her baby had finished her dinner. She was all cleaned up now and fast asleep. Suzanne was hoping to buy some uninterrupted conversation with Todd over dinner.

She walked through the living room and glanced out the front window. Totally dark out now. Still no sign of Todd. Maybe she'd take a minute in the bathroom and freshen up, see if she could erase some of the damage done by the day.

When she came out, she heard the garage door going up. Todd was probably starving by now. She certainly was. By the time she had the plates and drinks on the table, he was walking in.

"Sorry I'm late, again."

He looked weary and stressed out. She walked up and hugged him, held the hug a few moments longer. "Dinner's on the table."

He set his laptop bag on a chair next to the hutch. "I'll be right there."

He disappeared into their bedroom. She knew the routine. He had to lose the shirt and tie and the dress shoes before he could relax. She sat in her chair at the dining room table. Less than two minutes later, he joined her.

"This looks delicious." He led them in a quick prayer of thanks and began to eat. "How'd your day go?"

She hesitated to say, tried to think of something positive to start with. "Spent most of the afternoon running errands. The baby was unusually well behaved."

"That's good." He looked up from his plate. "Is anything wrong? Your eyes look, I don't know, sad."

"They are. I mean, I am a little sad. But we don't have to talk about it now."

He reached out his hand, rested it on hers. "Sure we do. Other than the traffic, which always drives me crazy, I had a pretty decent day. You can lean on me a little."

She set her fork down. "My dad called a little before lunch."

"Your dad? Not your mom?"

"He was calling about my mom."

"Is she all right? You just spoke with her a few days ago, right? On Thanksgiving?"

"Physically she's fine. But he said she's pretty depressed, worse than he's ever seen her."

"Really? Why?"

"I should've realized why on Thursday. This is the first year she and my dad spent Thanksgiving totally alone. None of us were there. And by the end of the day, she found out that none of us are coming for Christmas either."

"Hmm. Yeah, I guess that would do it, seeing how big your mom is about the holidays."

"She's even bigger about family and holidays," Suzanne said. They both took a few bites. She wasn't sure what to say about all this. They had already talked everything through last week when they'd made the decision that they couldn't afford to come home for either holiday this year.

"You know I wish we could go home for Christmas, right?" Todd said. "It really is only the money. I always enjoy hanging out with your folks."

"I know." It was nice of him to say. And she knew he meant it. And it wasn't like this move to Texas was something he'd forced her into. They both thought it would be a good idea.

At the time.

Now, six months later, she wasn't so sure. They both ate some more.

"Lately, I've been wondering if we made a mistake coming out here," Todd said.

"Really? Why?"

"Well, being so far away from the family is part of it. But I've been thinking about some other things. Like how tight our money is. It wasn't supposed to be like this. This transfer and new job paid three thousand more a year. The house prices between here and there are similar, so I knew *that* wouldn't cost more. I thought we might even save a little because the gas prices are so much cheaper."

"So why are things still so tight?" she asked.

"I never looked into the taxes," he said. "I saw that both Florida and Texas have no state income taxes, but Florida doesn't have them because they get the money from the tourists."

"What do they do here?"

"Looks like they get it from property taxes. We're paying almost two thousand a year more in property taxes."

"That's almost two-thirds of your raise eaten up right there."

"I know. And though the gas prices *are* cheaper, I'm actually spending several hundred dollars more a month than we did back home. It's twenty-five minutes farther to work than it used to be. And I wind up doubling the gas with all the stop-and-go traffic." He grabbed a chunk of pork chop with his fork and sighed.

"I'm sorry," she said. "I didn't know you were stressing out over the money."

"We're doing okay. I just thought we were going to be doing a lot better than okay. Truth is, if I'd known about these things, I might have just stayed put. This job is helping my resume some. It's definitely another rung up the ladder. Though right now it doesn't always feel worth it."

"Is there anything we can do? Are we stuck here for good?"

"For now we are. I had to agree to stay in this job for eighteen months before I can transfer out. That's a year from now. But I'm seriously thinking of keeping my eye out on the job board for transfers back to Florida about ten months from now."

"Really?"

"I can tell by the smile on your face, you like the sound of that."

"I don't hate it here, Todd. Not totally. I mean, I love our new church. I will definitely miss that. But I'm ready to go back to Florida whenever you are."

He reached over and squeezed her hand. "Hopefully, God

will open a door just about the time I'm freed up to start looking. But you know, with the money being tight again, that means we're really not going to be able to save anything for any trips back home."

"I know."

21

Several days had passed. Nothing much had changed in Judith's disposition, although after some continued prodding from Stan and Betty, she had decided to say yes to teaching that ornaments class at the craft store. She picked up the phone to call Betty.

"Well, hello," Betty said. "How are you doing this fine December morning?"

Judith had forgotten the calendar page had turned. "A little better." Which wasn't totally true.

"Given any more thought to teaching that class?"

"I have. I talked about it again last night with Stan. He thinks I should do it too. I guess I will."

"That's great. Have you called Doris?"

"Who's Doris?"

"I never told you her name? That's the craft store owner. I

went downtown yesterday to get my hair done, so I stopped in to see her. She remembered me. First thing she did was ask about you."

"I guess that means she's still interested," Judith said.

"I'd say she's a little more than interested."

"Why? What did she say?"

Betty hesitated. "Guess it's okay to tell you, now that you've decided to do it. She showed me the poster she's made to promote the class."

"She's made posters already? I haven't even told her I would do it."

"I know. She said if you said no, she'd just toss them out. But she had a lull this week and decided to make the posters up in case you said yes."

Well, sounded like she was serious then.

"So are you going to call her?"

"Do you know her number?"

"She has a website," Betty said. "I'm sure her number's on there."

"I could do that, but I think I'm just going to go down there. It's not that far, and if I'm going to do this, I should probably talk to her face-to-face. Besides, I need to look over what she has in terms of craft supplies so I can get an idea of the ornaments we might make in class."

"I like hearing you talk this way, Judith."

"I think it will probably do me some good. Get my mind off the things that are keeping me down."

"I think it's a great idea."

Judith wouldn't go that far. "Well, I'm ready to go. I just wanted to call you first."

"If you can, call me after with the details."

It was much easier to find a parking place today than it had been Saturday. Judith was able to park right on Donnelly Avenue, just a few doors down from the craft store.

The air was a bit cooler today than Saturday also. The weatherman had said a cold front was moving in and would probably drop the temperature into the low forties. Of course that would happen overnight when they were all asleep. But during the day tomorrow, she would need a light jacket if she ventured outdoors.

Judith walked down the sidewalk, nodding and smiling at a few passersby. As she approached the glass door, she began to tense up. She wasn't sure why. Once she was inside, she noticed a woman about her age near the front of the store. She looked up. Judith saw her name tag. It wasn't Doris; the tag said Marlene.

"Can I help you?"

"I'm looking for Doris. Is she in this morning?"

"Yes, she is. She's in the back doing some paperwork. May I tell her who's asking?"

"Sure. My name is Judith Winters, although I'm not sure she knows my name. I was in here Saturday with my friend Betty. That's who Doris talked with."

"Is she expecting you?"

"I don't think so. I'm here to talk with her about that mother-daughter craft class, the one about making ornaments from scratch."

"You are? We haven't really confirmed that we're having that class yet. How did you hear about it?"

"I'm the woman who's supposed to teach it. That is, if Doris still wants to have it."

A big smile came over Marlene's face. "Oh, she definitely does. And she'll definitely want to speak with you. Let me go get her." Marlene headed toward the back of the store.

Judith took a few more steps inside, partway down the craft supply aisle. A few moments later, both women came out. Doris extended her hand and shook Judith's warmly. Marlene excused herself, seeing a customer standing by the cash register.

"I'm so glad you've come back," Doris said. "Does this mean you decided to do it? To teach the class?"

"I have. I thought I should meet you in person, see what you have in mind."

Doris started walking down the aisle toward the back of the store. "Maybe we should talk down here, so you can see what's available. And you can let me know if there's anything you need."

Judith followed her. There was quite a selection. "I really like some of the ornaments I saw in the front half of the store when we were here last week. I'm guessing you'd like me to work with those?"

"That would be nice, since I have all the supplies for those. But only if you find ones you'd like the class to make. Your friend Betty said you've been making homemade ornaments with your kids for years. I'd be open to you making some of those, since you're already familiar with them. As long as I could get the materials." She made a face, like she was embarrassed about something. "And as long as they don't cost too much."

Judith realized money must be pretty tight for her. "I'm sure I can find some ornaments in here that'll work just fine. As long as I can figure out how to make them."

"I'm sure that won't be a problem," Doris said. "Most of them are pretty simple."

"So," Judith said, "where would we do the class?"

Doris pointed to an open space at the back of the store. "I thought right here. I don't have a separate room, but I thought we could just set a table up. There'll be some separation because it's in the back of the store, but I thought it might actually be nice that other customers could see it. It might stir some interest in the things you're making."

"I wouldn't have a problem doing it here," Judith said.

Doris turned toward the front of the store. "Why don't we go look at some of the finished ornaments, see what you think?" She led Judith down that aisle.

"Just so you know," Judith said as they walked, "none of the ornaments I made with my kids cost very much. Some of them didn't cost anything. My oldest daughter's favorite was just a big painted pinecone."

Doris laughed. "I'm not surprised. I think for the kids it's more about getting to spend that time with their mom and other kids their age, doing something fun." She stopped in front of the ornaments. "Well, here we are."

Judith looked them over, picked up several, and spun them around. They really were pretty simple. She doubted she'd have any problem figuring out how to make them or something similar using the materials Doris had in the back. But she also realized that although they were handmade, they were pretty polished looking. She thought again about Anna's blue pinecone, Brandon's snowman skeleton, and Suzanne's nativity aliens. Then about some of the other ornaments in that box.

"What's the matter?" Doris said. "You look a little concerned."

"It's nothing serious. At least I don't think it is."

"What is it?"

"It's just . . . I think I should make you aware of something, so we're both on the same page before we finalize anything."

"I think that's a good idea. Just share whatever you're thinking."

She picked up one of the nicer ornaments. "It's about expectations. What you expect, and maybe what some of the moms think we'll be able to make in my class."

"I'm not following you."

Judith held up the ornament. "Like this one. If I picked this one for the class, and even if I taught the kids the right way to make it, it may not look exactly like this when we were done."

"It wouldn't?"

Judith shook her head no.

"What would it look like?"

"To give you a clue, my husband Stan labeled our kids' homemade ornament box 'the ugly ornaments.' I like the kids to have fun, but I'm not a perfectionist. And sometimes the end result doesn't always turn out like we planned. Are you okay with that?"

Doris looked up at her. "I'm more than okay with it, Judith. It's perfect. Having fun and making memories is what it's all about."

22

Early the next morning, Stan and Barney were fishing on Lake Dora just after sunrise. Surprisingly, both had the morning off. The cold front had moved in overnight, so they wore jackets. Fortunately, the wind was calm and the water still as glass.

"I got a good feeling about this morning," Barney said. "These bass are hungry for breakfast."

"Think so, do ya?" Stan said.

"And I'm itching to try out this red rattle bait I bought at Bass Pro Shop last Friday."

Barney was in the back of the boat, holding the new lure in his hand. Stan was in the front, steering the electric trolling motor, which hardly made a sound. They had switched to the trolling motor because they were close to the water's edge and near their intended fishing spot. They didn't want to scare the fish away.

"Think that bait's gonna make a difference?" Stan asked. "It's the man holding the rod and reel, you ask me."

Barney smiled. He knew Stan had him with that one.

"Not sure you really believe that," Barney said. "Considering you were crediting this here bait the last time we were out."

"Well," Stan said, "guess this time we'll know for sure, won't we? Since we're both using the same bait." He said the last line in a loud whisper. "We better talk quieter. We're almost there."

Barney looked around. "Oh, right."

They rode the next few minutes in silence. Stan loved how quiet and peaceful it was out here on the water, especially in the morning. It was light enough to see where they were going but dark enough for several of the lakeside houses to still have their lights on.

"The GPS says we're there," Barney said.

Stan slowed the boat to a crawl, then shut it off and let them glide into some reeds. This was one of several fishing spots they'd worked over the years. One or both of them would always catch at least a fish or two here. After a few casts, things got pretty quiet. A picture of Judith came to Stan's mind. When he had gotten home from work yesterday, she had seemed as down as she'd been on Thanksgiving. She hadn't even plugged in the Christmas tree lights all day. In the past, that was the first thing she'd do every morning during the Christmas season, even before starting the coffee.

Over dinner, he'd asked her about how her day had gone. Come to find out, she'd decided to go ahead and teach that ornament class downtown, like he and Betty had suggested.

Stan was glad to hear it and told her so. But she hadn't shown any excitement about it while they talked. No more than when she talked about doing the laundry.

Stan thought about the big boat parade tomorrow night. It was one of the annual Christmas events held every year in Mount Dora. Dozens of boats, all lit up with Christmas lights, paraded by on the waterfront downtown. He and Judith went every year. He was thinking about suggesting they go again this year but wasn't sure it was a good idea. Last week at the Light Up celebration, all she seemed to focus on were the memories of previous years when all the kids and grandkids were there to enjoy it. Would that happen again if they went to the boat parade?

He tried to shut all this out of his mind. It just confused him. She confused him. He didn't understand why she couldn't accept things the way they were. Kids grow up. They move out, start their own lives. He would've liked to see them all at Christmastime too. Though it was nice having a quiet Thanksgiving. But there was nothing to be done about it. Those three phone calls to his kids confirmed it. She had to let it go, or it was just gonna tear her up inside and wind up making them both miserable.

"Are you gonna fish or not?"

Stan looked up at Barney.

"That spinnerbait's just sitting there dead in the water. No bass is gonna hit that."

"All right. Hold your horses."

Just then, there was a splash and Barney's rod bent almost in half. "Here we go," he said, snapping the rod back to set the hook. "Feels like it's got some size."

"You want me to get the net?"

"Give me a minute." He continued to wrestle the fish as he reeled it in. "I think I got it."

As it neared the boat, the fish splashed some more. Stan could see the silver of its side just beneath the water's surface. "Looks like at least a two-pounder."

"Some good eating then," Barney said through gritted teeth.

"We ate the bass we caught last Friday for dinner last night. Judith panfried 'em in a garlic and lemon butter sauce."

Barney finally brought the bass to the side of the boat and lifted it over the edge. It was definitely a keeper. After Stan removed the red rattle bait from its mouth, Barney lifted the lid to the livewell and set her in.

"So, whaddya think?" Stan asked. "Did you catch that fish or was it the new lure?"

Barney spun around in his chair, smiled. "A little of both, I guess." He checked the bait over, then cast it out again.

Stan cast his bait out again too. As it plunked in the water, they heard the unmistakable sound of a motorboat cruising by behind them, maybe about a hundred yards away.

Barney turned first. "Well, would you look at that? Stan, you gotta see this."

Stan spun halfway around in his seat.

"That's almost exactly like our boat," Barney said. "Our dream rig."

"I think you're right." There were two guys inside. "That's gonna be us," Stan said. "In just a few weeks. Hard to imagine."

Barney reeled his lure in the last few feet, then cast it out again. "Not for me. I imagine it all the time. I was thinking about it this morning as we lowered this baby in the water.

And as I stepped into it, and it rocked back and forth like it always does. And I thought about our dream rig, how sturdy it's gonna be. Solid as the dock."

The boat sailed out of view. "It's gonna be nice."

"So nice." Barney cast out again. "Seeing that boat reminded me of something I wanted to talk to you about."

"What's that?"

"I had an idea. Something I've been thinking about for a week or so."

"Okay."

"You know they got that big bass fishing tournament in the Harris chain of lakes the week between Christmas and New Year."

"I recall something about that." People from all over participated in it every year. Barney and Stan had never given it a serious thought before. They wouldn't be caught dead in a prestigious event like that in this old thing.

"It only costs a hundred dollars to enter. The winner walks away with thousands. It falls on the twenty-seventh this year, two days after Christmas. We'll have our dream rig by then."

"You think we should enter? You think we have a chance?"

"I think so. We do pretty good in this piece of junk. Think of how we'll do fishing in a boat like the one that just went by, with all that new equipment. It's a three-bass open tournament. So it's the size, not the quantity. And it's open to anyone. You don't have to be a member of any club."

Stan thought a minute.

Barney continued. "But there's another aspect of this idea. I'm thinking if we pick up our boat on Christmas Day, or even the day after, that won't leave us any time to try it out, to work out the kinks."

"You think our dream rig's going to have kinks?"

"I don't think the boat will, but you and I will. We won't know what the heck we're doing. I don't think we have a chance of winning that tournament if we don't get some time in the boat before it starts."

"So what do you suggest?"

"I suggest we come up with the money three or four days before Christmas and take possession of it then. That way we'll be able to go out at least once or twice before the tournament."

That was a great idea.

"I know I'll have my share of the money before then," Barney said. "Almost have it all together now. Can you be ready a few days early with your part?"

"I should have it all by then," Stan said. "I'll have to crunch the numbers to make sure."

"Then why don't you do that?" Barney said. "And I'll find out what's involved in registering for this tournament."

23

Taryn Simpson was finishing up her caramel macchiato at her favorite coffee shop on Donnelly Avenue when her friend Samantha happened by. Samantha was inside now getting her coffee. Taryn was sitting at an outdoor table. She was happy to see Samantha, but she didn't plan on staying very long. Her daughter Madison's school let out in ten minutes.

Taryn glanced at the front door. No sign of Samantha yet. She looked around at the other customers sitting outside and her thoughts returned, once again, to the topic she had been pondering before Samantha showed up. Taryn was the only person here whose face wasn't glued to some kind of electronic screen. IPads, smartphones, laptops, you name it. Before Thanksgiving Day, she'd probably have joined right in.

She had a smartphone but deliberately left it in her purse,

refusing to look at it the entire time she was here. To help, she'd turned the volume off. The front door opened and Samantha walked out, all smiles. Taryn looked at her watch. She couldn't lose track of the time.

Samantha said, "You have to go?"

"In a few minutes. Gotta pick up Maddie from school."

Samantha sat beside her. "What are you thinking about?"

"What do you mean?"

"When I came out, you were looking all around with this look on your face."

Taryn smiled. "Okay, something's been bothering me lately, ever since Thanksgiving Day."

"What is it?"

Taryn lowered her voice. "Look around at all the people here. What's the one thing they have in common?"

Samantha sipped her drink as she eyed the other patrons. A few moments later, she said, "I give up. Whatever it is, I'm not seeing it. I see men and women here, of various ages, wearing different colors and different styles of clothes. What am I missing?"

Taryn pointed to the smartphone that Samantha had set next to her drink, faceup. "That," she said. "Your phone. Everyone here is looking at their phones. I noticed it inside, the same thing. Only some are using laptops in there. But no one's talking. No one's visiting or having any interaction with anyone else."

Just then Samantha's phone vibrated. She reached for it.

"Don't you dare," Taryn said.

Samantha turned her phone upside down on a napkin. "It's no big deal. It's just the way people communicate now. Why does it bother you?"

"Because I remember how it used to be just a few years ago when people weren't like this. Back in the dumb phone days and before people had iPads. To go online you had to sit by your computer at home. Now we're connected all the time, but no one pays any attention to the people they're with."

Samantha looked around again. "What started you off on this tirade?"

"I'm not on a tirade, it's just starting to bother me."

"You said 'ever since Thanksgiving' a second ago. What happened on Thanksgiving?"

"We all showed up to my parents' house, like we do every year. All the kids and grandkids, my aunt and uncle. After my dad prayed, he announced a rule, no cell phones at the table. I realized a few hours later that was the only time we actually talked to each other the whole day. At one point, a whole bunch of us were sitting around the family room, and every single person—including me—were on our smartphones. The kids were all playing games on their iPads or some other touchscreen tablet. No one said a word. We were all lost in our own little worlds. For some reason, right then, it just really stuck out to me how wrong it is."

"Did you say anything?"

"I did but in a joking way. No one picked up on it. So I got up and forced myself out to the patio to join the older relatives, who were actually visiting and getting caught up. I decided I don't want to live with this addiction anymore."

"Addiction . . . listen to you. You're kidding, right?" Samantha took another sip.

"Kind of, but not really. I think it's kind of an addiction. It's like I have to constantly keep checking my phone, see if anybody's tried to contact me. Check for texts, check my email, check Twitter, check Facebook. There's always something there. And usually, it's nothing important. But I treat it like it is and instantly respond. Then it starts all over again." Taryn set her coffee down. "The worst part, to me, is the kids. Maddie included. They should've been outside playing. But every single one of them was on some kind of a device. The only physical activity going on was their fingers swiping the screen."

Samantha laughed. "It's sad but true. I was reading an article in a woman's magazine this past weekend highlighting all the dangers of giving kids all these electronic devices when they're so young. The article quoted some study that said it's shutting down kids' creativity and warping their communication skills."

"I'm just as guilty," Taryn said. "Maddie's been using one for several years now. She's on hers all the time. I realized I've been using it like a babysitter. It keeps her occupied and lets me get some things done around the house. But not this week. I started limiting her time to one hour, twice a day."

"How's that working out?"

"I won't lie, it's been a struggle. She's pitched a fit a few times. But I figured out what the struggle is. Mostly it's me. Now I have to spend time with her doing old-fashioned, nonelectronic things. But if I'm doing things with her, I have less time to do things I want to do. But that's okay. Being a mom's not supposed to be easy, right? It has been kind of tricky coming up with old-fashioned things we can do together. But I'm determined to make this work."

"Old-fashioned moms have done it for generations," Samantha said. "I'm sure you'll figure something out."

Taryn looked at her watch again. "Well, I've gotta pick Maddie up from school. It's been great bumping into you."

"You too, Taryn." Samantha got a funny look on her face. "I just thought of something you and Maddie can do together. Something very old-fashioned and definitely not electronic."

Taryn stood. "What?"

Samantha stood also and started walking toward the front door of the coffee shop.

"Where are you going?"

"Follow me. It'll just take a sec. It's a little flyer I saw taped to the glass near the front window. A mother-daughter class."

Taryn picked up her purse and followed her.

"Here it is," Samantha said. "It's at that craft store down the road."

Taryn began to read. This was perfect. A mother-daughter craft class making homemade Christmas ornaments together on Saturday mornings. She had Saturdays off. "I like this. I think Maddie will too. Thanks, Sam." She reached into her purse and pulled out her phone.

"You going to call her?"

"No, taking a picture of the flyer."

24

Taryn was happy to find an open angled parking space on Donnelly Avenue just a few doors down from the craft store she planned to visit. She was terrible at parallel parking, which was the only kind available on the other side of the street.

"After we visit this store," her daughter Maddie said from the passenger seat, "*then* can I play with my tablet again?"

Taryn looked at her, tried to keep her composure. Seeing Maddie's withdrawal symptoms, Taryn did not think *addiction* was too strong a word in her conversation with Samantha. She took a deep, calming breath. "Maddie, you can when we get home. It's not even in the car anyway."

"You didn't bring it?"

"No, I didn't bring it. And if you decide to use it right when we get home, your new time allowance will start then."

"We're still doing that?"

"Yes, we're still doing that. And your attitude right now is helping me see how important it is to keep doing that."

Maddie looked away, folded her arms in protest.

"Maddie . . ." Taryn waited. "Maddie, look at me." She waited some more. Maddie finally turned her head and faced her mother. "I know this feels like a punishment to you, but cutting back the amount of time you can play on that thing—"

"It *is* a punishment."

"No, it's not. I'm trying to help you."

"Help me? How is taking away my favorite thing to do helping me? Especially when I haven't done anything wrong."

Taryn didn't know if she could explain this, at least in a way a modern seven-year-old would understand. "I'm the one who's done something wrong, and now I'm trying to fix it."

"If you did something wrong, how come I'm the one being punished?"

"You're not being punished, Maddie."

"Feels like it."

"It may feel like it. But, believe me, you're not. It's for your own good." Taryn thought a moment. "It's like your bedtime. If your father and I didn't make you go to bed at eight thirty on school nights, how late would you stay up?"

"I don't know. A lot later than that."

"Right, and then you'd be miserable in the morning and probably fall asleep in class. But you know what happens every night . . . around nine o'clock?"

"What?"

"Either I or your father quietly open your bedroom door and check on you. And you know what we find, every night

131

without fail?" Maddie shook her head. "We find you . . . sound asleep. And you know what that shows? That shows you need us to set boundaries for you. That's how God set things up. All little kids need boundaries until they're old enough to make the right decisions on their own."

Maddie unfolded her arms. "You're saying cutting how much I can play on my tablet is like my bedtime?"

"That's what I'm saying."

"But everyone else gets to play on their tablets as much as they want."

"They're not my little girl. You are. And I know I used to let you do it as much as you wanted, but I was wrong. And because of my mistake, you don't even know how to play the way you used to, with regular kid toys." Taryn pointed toward the craft store through the windshield. "And that's why I stopped here today. I found out about a mother-daughter class they're teaching at that craft store over there. I thought we could check it out, see if it's something you and I would like to do together."

"We would make crafts? You and me? What kind?" She was actually smiling.

"I'm not sure. Why don't we go in and find out? I saw a flyer in a window a little while ago. It said something about making ornaments."

"Christmas ornaments?"

Taryn nodded. "Would you like that?"

Maddie nodded. "But we haven't even set our tree up yet."

"We're going to do that soon."

"When?"

"Soon." Taryn's husband had been traveling a lot the last few weeks. "I'll talk to your father tonight, and we'll pick a night we know he's going to be home. You want him to help us, right?"

"Yes."

"Wouldn't it be fun if we can hang some ornaments we made ourselves?"

Maddie's face lit up.

"So, let's go check it out."

With both of their moods improved, Taryn and Maddie walked down the sidewalk toward the craft store. Maddie even reached for her mother's hand. When they reached the front door, Taryn saw the same flyer about the ornament class taped to the window and pointed it out to Maddie. Once inside, Taryn bent down and whispered, "I'm going to go see about this class. You can look around, but stay away from the door and be careful about what you pick up. If it's breakable, you probably should just look and not touch."

"I'll be careful."

Taryn looked around the store. She spotted two women with name tags talking to other customers. She walked toward the woman in the back. She seemed to be speaking with more authority. Maybe she was the owner. As Taryn got closer, she noticed the women were standing by a long rectangular table. Spread out across the table were a variety of different craft supplies. A woman without a name badge held a clipboard and was writing things down. Did she work here too?

Taryn didn't want to be rude, so she stood off to the side and looked through some craft items on the shelves. An easy distraction. They were all about Christmas.

A few moments later, a woman's voice behind her said, "Is there anything I can help you with?"

Taryn turned. "I hope so."

"My name is Doris. I'm the store owner. I see you're browsing through our make-it-yourself section. Are you interested in making crafts?"

Taryn glanced down the aisle, saw Maddie looking at a stuffed reindeer. "I'm not much of a craft person. I mean, I like them. I just don't know how to make them. But I saw your poster about a mother-daughter class." Doris's smile instantly got wider. Taryn noticed the woman with the clipboard was now looking her way. "I've been looking for something to do with my daughter. Something that doesn't involve electronics or swiping your finger across a screen."

Doris laughed. "Well, you've come to the right place. The only finger swiping going on around here might be to wipe some Elmer's glue off on a napkin." She turned as the woman with the clipboard walked up. "And you've also come at the right time. It just so happens the teacher of the class is here. This is Judith Winters."

Taryn shook her hand. "You're teaching the ornaments class?"

"I am."

"We just started promoting it yesterday," Doris said. "Customers have been asking about it all day."

"Is there still time to sign up?"

"We have a few spots left." Doris pointed at the table. "This is where Judith will be teaching. As you can see, it's not a huge space, so we'll have to go with first come, first served."

"Well, we definitely want to sign up. Let me get my daughter, Maddie." Taryn hurried down the aisle. Maddie was now holding some funny-looking elves. "C'mon, Maddie, there's someone I want you to meet."

"Who?" She took hold of Taryn's hand and followed her to the back of the store.

"The woman who will be teaching us how to make ornaments." She brought her to the two ladies.

Judith set her clipboard on the table and bent down to shake Maddie's hand. "How do you do, young lady. What's your name?"

"Maddie. It's short for Madison."

"That's a beautiful name. And how old are you?"

"Seven. I'm in second grade now."

"That's a wonderful age. My oldest granddaughter is seven."

"Will she be taking the class?"

Judith smiled. "No, she lives far away in a state called Virginia. But if she lived here, I'm sure she'd want to meet you."

Doris looked at Taryn. "You probably saw on the flyer, there's no charge for the class. The only cost will be buying the materials used to make the ornaments. That's why Judith came down today, to look over what we have and decide which ornaments she's going to teach the kids to make. I need to make sure I have everything because the class starts next Saturday."

"Next Saturday," Taryn said. "Good. I was hoping it wasn't tomorrow, because we already have other plans. I don't want to miss the first class."

"You're just in time," Doris said.

"Say," Judith said, still looking at Maddie. "I have an idea. We'll have two Saturdays left before Christmas to do the classes. My goal is for the kids to make one ornament each class."

"Do we get to keep them?" Maddie asked.

"You certainly do," Judith said. "And you can help me make a decision. I've been thinking about the ornaments I'd like the kids to make. We only have time to make two. I've picked out one. But I'm having a hard time deciding which of the other two I like better. Can I show them to you, and you tell me which one's your favorite?"

Maddie nodded yes. Taryn already loved this lady.

Judith led her to the table and showed her the two ornaments she had in mind. "Look them over. Take your time. And tell me which one is your favorite."

Maddie went back and forth between the two, then finally pointed to the same one Taryn was looking at: a cute little reindeer made from wine corks and pipe cleaners.

"I like that one. Good choice," Judith said.

Taryn looked at Doris and said, "Where do we sign up?"

25

Tomorrow morning was Judith's first ornament-making class at the craft store. She was a little nervous, but not about making the ornaments themselves. Doris had given her the materials to practice at home last weekend. Now Judith could make them in her sleep. They were really quite simple.

She was more nervous about teaching the class, interacting with the parents and kids. How would she do? Would she be able to explain things easily? Would they be disappointed after? Teaching was something she used to be good at, and loved. She had gotten her degree in elementary education and taught school for several years before her kids were born. But she and Stan had decided she'd be a stay-at-home mom, so the last time she had taught a class with kids was over thirty years ago.

Before he had left for work, Stan had seen her fiddling

with the ornaments at the dining room table and asked her if she was excited about teaching the class tomorrow. All she could manage was a long pause. He'd asked what was wrong, so she told him.

"Haven't taught kids for thirty years?" he repeated back to her. "What are you talking about? You taught Anna, Brandon, and Suzanne everything they know."

But this was different. That was just life, a mom with her kids. Classroom teaching was different.

Her phone rang. Her eyes scanned the living room until she found it sitting on the end table closest to the Christmas tree. She picked it up and noticed that the Christmas tree lights were still off. There was the green plug lying on the floor near the socket. That was the last thing Stan had said before walking out the door: "Don't forget to plug in the tree."

Looking at the screen, she saw it was Suzanne, which instantly made her smile. "Good morning. How are things in Texas?"

"Things are freezing cold in Texas," Suzanne said. "I'm not sure I'll ever get used to the wind here. It blows so much stronger. You know when they say 'wind chill factor,' well, that really matters here."

"Are you staying warm?"

"Trying to. We had our first cold snap the week before Thanksgiving. It was obvious then our Florida winter coats weren't going to cut it. Todd took us out to buy some new ones, but I don't know. I walked down the driveway this morning to bring an empty trash can back into the garage, and that wind started kicking up. It blew right through me."

"We're in the middle of a cold front here," Judith said. "Forced your dad to wear a sweater to work this morning."

Suzanne laughed. "Maybe you'll see some snow on the mountain before it's over."

That made Judith chuckle. Suzanne was referring to *Mount* Dora.

"Speaking of snow on the mountain," Suzanne said, "isn't tomorrow when they bring all that snow into Donnelly Park? I used to love going to that every year."

"It is." Every year, the city filled the hill behind the Donnelly Center with snow, making little runs for the kids to sled down. They'd line the runs with hay bales and place more hay at the bottom where the snow ended.

"Are you and Dad going?"

"I guess so," Judith said. "We haven't really talked about it."

"You should. It'll be fun."

"Any chance you guys will see some real snow out there?" Judith knew that was one of the things Suzanne had hoped to see, moving to Texas. It didn't snow often, only averaged two inches a year, but last year the man who'd hired Todd said one time it snowed six inches and the snow stayed on the ground for three days.

"There's no snow in the forecast so far. Just freezing temperatures and ridiculously cold wind."

Judith was just about to ask her if she regretted moving out there but held her peace. For the next several minutes, Suzanne filled her in on what had been happening since they last spoke. How Todd's job was coming along, how much she enjoyed their new and very big church. Judith especially enjoyed hearing all the stories about the baby.

But hearing all this also stirred afresh the sadness in Judith's heart that she wasn't able to see these things for herself.

And she wouldn't see them in the days left between now and Christmas or on Christmas Day.

Suzanne must've detected her declining mood. At one point she stopped and asked, "So, how are you doing with all this? You and dad being alone for the holidays?"

Judith thought a moment. When she lived here, Suzanne had become more a friend than a daughter, almost a confidante. But Judith couldn't open up about this. It wouldn't be right. It was too close to being manipulative, something she vowed she'd never be. But she couldn't lie either. Suzanne would see right through it. "I have good days and bad days," she said. She instantly realized that was very close to a lie. She wasn't having any good days lately.

"What kind of day is this?" Suzanne asked.

"I don't know. Too early to tell."

"Are you and Dad doing anything different this year?"

"I don't think so. Your dad helped me decorate the house and the tree. That was different."

"You know, Mom, I was reading an article in a magazine yesterday. It caught my eye because it talked about people in your and Dad's situation."

"Our situation?" Judith thought she knew what Suzanne meant but wasn't sure.

"Empty nesters at Christmastime. It was about things to do to replace all the family traditions when the kids move out. It had lots of good ideas, new things I thought you could try. I checked into it, and the magazine has an online version of the article. Want me to send you the link?"

"Sure. Speaking of new things . . . I'm teaching a class. It starts tomorrow."

"You are? What kind of class?"

Judith told her about the ornaments class at the craft store.

When she finished, Suzanne said, "That's so exciting, Mom. I'm so proud of you stepping out of your comfort zone like that."

"It's definitely a stretch for me."

"I'm sure you'll do a great job. I have such good memories of making ornaments. Brianna's a little too young right now, but that's one tradition I definitely want to keep going in my house."

That was nice to hear.

"I was actually thinking about asking you if I could have a few of them when we moved out here. The ugly ornaments, as Dad called them. But I know how special they are to you, so I never brought it up."

That stung a little. Not that Suzanne thought of asking for the ornaments. It was the pain that went along with the memory of seeing the ornaments the day after Thanksgiving. She thought about the moment two weeks ago when she had shown them to Betty. Now they were just sitting up in the attic. She hoped Suzanne didn't ask whether they were hanging on the tree. "I wouldn't mind if you wanted some of them," Judith said. "Remember which ones you made?"

"Every single one."

"Well, if you want a few of them, just let me know which ones. I could probably ship them out to you before Christmas."

"Really?"

"Really," Judith said. "I don't mind parting with a few of them." Or perhaps with all of them.

"Okay . . . well, I'll think about it then. And be checking

your email. I know you don't look at it very often. But I'll send you that link to the magazine article."

After hanging up the phone, Suzanne began to picture some of the "ugly ornaments" she and her mom had been talking about. Of course, she thought of her favorite: the one her dad had nicknamed the alien nativity ornament. She remembered how deeply offended she was the moment he'd first said it. As she'd gotten older, she was able to see for herself the nickname had been properly earned.

Jesus, Mary, and Joseph did look like aliens. Thinking about it now made her smile.

She was surprised her mom had so quickly offered to let them go, even ship them to her in Texas. Her mom had treasured those ornaments and had spoken of them as more valuable than almost anything she owned. Suzanne remembered one conversation they'd had after watching a news story about a house that had burned down. They began to discuss the kinds of things they would grab on the way out if their own house caught fire. Her mom had said only two things mattered: her photo albums and family videos and that box of ugly ornaments. Everything else, she had said, the insurance could replace. Now her mom was ready to send them to Suzanne without a moment's hesitation.

What did it mean?

She was afraid it was another symptom of her mom's growing holiday depression, and as much as Suzanne would love to get some of those ornaments, she wasn't entirely sure it had been a wise thing to ask for them.

26

Judith parked her car on a side street off Donnelly Avenue, a short walk to the craft store. She had prayed that morning for God to give her a clear head and a peaceful heart, so she could teach this ornaments class well and make it fun for the moms and daughters.

The peaceful heart had lasted from that moment until now. As she turned off the car, the peace suddenly disappeared. As she walked down the sidewalk, the clear head was also gone, replaced by a barrage of conflicting thoughts. Which ornament should she teach first? How should she introduce the lesson? How should she introduce herself? What should she have the kids do? What should she have the moms do? What if no one else signed up to take the class?

When she reached the corner, she froze. For a moment, she thought about turning around and heading back to the car. But then she saw a mother and daughter hand in hand walking toward the craft store. Both smiling widely. The little girl's eyes were lit up with joy. Then Judith recognized them as the mother and daughter she had met when she was finalizing the details with Doris. They saw her and waved. She waved back and continued walking forward.

"Good morning," she said. What were their names again? She used to be so good at remembering names. Name tags. She should have gotten name tags. That would've solved the problem. It was too late now.

"Good morning to you," the mother said. "Maddie is so excited about the class. She hasn't talked about anything else since we left the store."

Judith held the door open. Maddie, her name was Maddie. "And I'm so glad you came back." She glanced at her watch. The class didn't start for ten minutes. The store had only been open for twenty. The downtown area was already busy with early-morning shoppers, but Judith only saw a few customers in the store. Doris stood behind the counter. When she saw Judith, Maddie, and Maddie's mother she instantly smiled and began walking toward them.

"Isn't this exciting?" she said to all three.

Maddie and her mother responded with an enthusiastic yes. Judith nodded. They walked toward the back of the store. When they arrived, Judith observed that all the supplies for one of the ornaments—the cork reindeer—were laid out around the table in little plastic trays. Apparently, Doris had decided which ornament she should teach first. That was easy. Seeing so many trays laid out this way prompted her to ask, "Did this many people sign up?"

"They certainly did. We actually had to start a waiting

list." Doris looked at Maddie and her mother. "Since you're here first, you get to pick wherever you want to sit."

Judith leaned toward Doris and said, "You wouldn't have name tags in the store by any chance, would you?"

A surprised look came over Doris's face. "Name tags. I thought about that. I just forgot to set them out. Let me go get them."

Judith breathed a sigh of relief. She walked to the front of the table and set her purse on the chair, laid her notebook on the table. She turned to the pages she'd written about the little cork reindeer. Two more mothers and daughters arrived. Judith introduced herself and encouraged them to find a seat.

Doris quickly came back with a small stack of name tags and a black marker. Over the next few minutes, three more mothers arrived with their daughters, filling up all the spots at the table. Doris stood next to Judith and welcomed them all and introduced Judith to the class. She pointed out the name tags and asked for them to pass them around and for everyone to put one on. Then she explained about the materials in the little trays in front of them and pointed out a small, itemized list underneath the trays showing the cost for everything they were about to make.

Most of the moms, at this point, peeked at the bottom line and smiled. Judith knew they would. Doris had made this a very inexpensive project. She then added, "Of course, once Judith shows you how to make these cute little cork reindeer, you may want to make several more of them as Christmas gifts for friends and family."

She turned to Judith and said, "What would you like the class to call you?"

Judith smiled. "I suppose the moms could just call me

Judith and their daughters could call me Miss Judith." Judith looked at the members of the class. She glanced down at Maddie's mother's name tag. Taryn. That's right, her name was Taryn.

After all the introductory comments were said and everyone had gone around the table introducing themselves to each other, Judith held up the finished product: a cute little reindeer made mostly of wine corks and pipe cleaners. She passed it around.

"Everyone take a good look at it," she said. "You'll notice that the individual pieces that make up this little guy are all sitting in front of you. I'll show you how to put them all together so that yours looks something like this when we're through."

Maddie held up a sheet of waxed paper covered with evenly spaced white dots. "Miss Judith, what's this for?"

"That's a good question, Maddie. Class, why don't each of you pull out that paper full of dots that Maddie's holding on to. These are called glue dots. When making crafts, we're always going to be gluing things together. Normally, when I glue something, I use a hot glue gun. They have them here, and some of you girls might be old enough to use one. But I thought to be safe, and a little less messy, we'd use these glue dots. They're very easy to use. I'll show you how in just a few minutes."

She held up a knife with a black plastic handle. "I thought I should also mention this. When making crafts, occasionally we have to cut things in half or make shorter things out of longer things. When that happens, we'll use a knife like this or maybe an X-Acto knife. But the blades on these are very sharp and could cut you badly if you slip and make a mistake. Until your mom says you're old enough, never cut things by yourself."

She held up the finished reindeer. "See his legs here? They're actually made from two corks cut in half, to make four pieces. You already have those four pieces in your trays." She pointed to the brown antlers. "These are made from brown pipe cleaners. And see the reindeer's ears? They're made by looping little strands of jute, or twine." Judith paused and smiled as she watched the moms and daughters all going through their trays, picking out all the different pieces and holding them up.

This wasn't going too badly, she thought. Everyone seemed to be enjoying themselves. She looked to her right and noticed a small crowd of customers standing down the aisles, watching and listening. She glanced back at the counter and saw Doris, who smiled and nodded her approval.

Maybe she could do this. Maybe Judith hadn't lost her touch after all.

27

Maddie had been so excited about her creation ever since the ornament class ended this morning. She'd wanted to hang it on the tree so badly, all afternoon, but Taryn had asked her to wait until her father came home this evening. Tim had just called saying he was less than five minutes away.

Taryn looked at Maddie peeking through the front window, holding her little cork reindeer in her hand. She was so proud of it. And Taryn couldn't be happier about the way things had turned out. That class had to be one of the most fun times they'd ever had together. Perhaps the best part of all: Maddie hadn't asked to play with her tablet since they'd arrived home.

Taryn sat on her favorite side of the sofa listening to soft Christmas music playing in the background. She had already switched off the lamp beside her, allowing the family Christmas tree to glimmer and radiate its light throughout the room. That was the scene Tim liked to come home to during the holiday season, especially when he'd been on a trip. She smiled as she pondered another scene about to unfold when he got home, once he saw Maddie's cork reindeer.

How would he react?

Because this glimmering, shimmering family Christmas tree was Tim's baby, a true work of art, as elegant and beautiful as any tree she'd seen in the Christmas issues of *Woman's Day* or *Southern Living* magazine.

In one of those shocking revelations married couples discover that first year, Taryn had found out she'd married a Christmas snob. At least where the Christmas tree was concerned.

Tim had handled the situation tactfully that first year. Over a latte and a shared slice of pumpkin cheesecake at their favorite café, he had asked Taryn to share her favorite Christmas traditions growing up. So she did. He'd listened carefully and had even asked follow-up questions. When she'd finished, he'd pointed out that she hadn't mentioned any traditions involving the tree. She'd told him they had always set one up, and she'd always enjoyed decorating it, but she didn't recall any specific traditions about the tree itself.

A big smile had come over his face as he'd said, "In our home, if we follow all your favorite traditions, would you be okay if I got to take charge of the tree?" It had seemed an odd thing to ask at the time, but she had no serious objection. He'd made it clear they could decorate it together; he'd just like to pick out the tree, the kind of lights, the ornaments, and where they'd go.

She was used to it now, but it had been almost comical to watch how he'd pulled the project together that first Christmas. The meticulous care and level of detail he brought to the effort. She'd never thought of decorating the Christmas tree as serious business before. But she had to admit . . . the end result was spectacular. Everyone who visited their home said it was the most beautiful Christmas tree they had ever seen.

That year and every year since.

They had set up this year's tree together Thursday evening after dinner. Thankfully, Tim always made it a fun evening. As fun as possible, considering. Things never got tense, probably because Taryn deferred to Tim as the lead decorator and more or less served as his assistant. She paid attention to how he did things and the way he liked them. Most of the time, she guessed it right. It wasn't that big a sacrifice. To her, it was no different than how he deferred to her leadership in the kitchen when she was cooking a holiday meal.

The funnier thing was watching him with Maddie.

Of course, Maddie didn't flow with the program. Kids as a rule never did. She was walking by her second Christmas and definitely wanted to help out. Tim was very patient with her, taking the time to hand her specific ornaments and point right to where they should go on the tree. He'd turn around and go back for more ornaments, and she would stick her ornament anywhere she pleased. But he never yelled. He never even moved it back to its proper place. Not in front of her anyway; he'd wait until she went to bed.

As she'd gotten older, Tim had trained her well. She rarely made a mistake.

But now Maddie was holding an ornament made of cork and pipe cleaners that looked handmade. Taryn looked back at the tree. Every single ornament was store-bought. But not just store-bought; the majority of them were collectibles. Some fairly expensive. None of these thoughts had occurred to her when she signed them up to take this ornaments class. She was only concerned with finding something normal and nonelectronic they could do together.

Headlights flashed through the front window curtains.

"He's home, Mommy. Daddy's home."

Taryn stood. "I see that. I know you're excited about your reindeer, but give him a minute to get in the door."

"I will. Do you think after dinner we could go sledding at Donnelly Park?"

"Maybe, if Daddy's not too worn out."

"He said we could before he went on his trip. He said, 'When I get home Saturday, I'll take you sledding.'"

"Then I'm sure he will. But don't bring it up right away. Let's talk about it at dinner."

Maddie walked to a spot about ten feet from the front door. She put her hands, including the one holding the reindeer, behind her back.

Taryn came up and stood behind her. She heard the car turn off. Tim would be in a generally good mood; she knew this from the earlier phone call. He'd been on a short business trip to Atlanta since yesterday morning. Apparently, things had gone better than expected.

The door unlocked and swung open.

"I'm home," he said, stepping inside the foyer. He set his brief bag down and rolled his carry-on suitcase off to the side. Bending, he opened his arms, and Maddie ran straight into them. She hugged and kissed him, still clinging to her reindeer.

He stood, still holding Maddie. Taryn kissed and hugged him from the other side.

"Now this is what I've been waiting for all day." After closing the front door, they took a few steps onto the carpet. He sniffed the air. "Smells good. What's for dinner?"

"Chicken divan," Taryn said.

"With extra divan?" he asked, meaning extra curry.

"Of course."

He set Maddie down, walked a few steps farther, and stopped in front of the tree. Maddie came up right behind him. He put his arm around her. "Two weeks to Christmas."

"I know. I can't wait."

He looked at Taryn. "I took Monday off, if you want to do a little more Christmas shopping while Maddie's at school."

"I'd love to."

He looked down at Maddie, who had the reindeer ornament behind her back again. She was moving sideways back and forth and wore a mischievous smile.

"Is something going on? Something I don't know about?" He looked up at Taryn.

"Not with me," she said. "Ask Maddie."

He bent down. That's when he noticed her hands behind her back. "What have you got back there?"

"A surprise."

"A surprise? For me?"

She nodded. "It's kind of like a present too."

"A present? Don't I have to wait until Christmas?"

"Not with this one. It's something you're supposed to have between now and Christmas."

"What is it?"

"Something I made at a store today with Mommy."

"Something you made. What is it? Let's see it."

"Close your eyes."

He did.

"No peeking."

"I'm not peeking."

"Okay . . ." She pulled the reindeer from behind her back and dangled it in front of his face. "Okay. You can open them."

He did. It took a moment for his eyes to focus on the ornament. He smiled immediately. For a moment, Taryn was afraid that smile would turn into a laugh. In class that morning, Mrs. Winters had urged all the moms not to worry about how the ornament turned out. It was just supposed to be a fun time. It certainly was that. Looking at it now, through Tim's eyes, the poor reindeer's flaws stood out quite a bit.

One of its brown pipe cleaner antlers was considerably smaller than the other. The eyes weren't spaced symmetrically apart, giving the reindeer the appearance of being cross-eyed. Maddie had accidentally glued the two back legs way too far apart. The reindeer looked like it was slipping on ice.

But one look in Tim's eyes took away all her fears. They were welling up with tears. "You made this for me?"

She nodded. "Yep. Just for you. Do you like it?"

"Like it? I love it." He threw his arms around her and squeezed her tight.

Taryn reached down and gently stroked the side of his face.

He released Maddie from the hug and took the ornament from her.

"Where should we put it on the tree?" she said.

Tim stood and turned around, facing the tree. "I know right where it should go."

What he did next brought a tear to Taryn's eyes. He took his favorite ornament—his previously favorite ornament—a very expensive collectible he'd bought in Florence on their honeymoon, from its front-and-center place of honor on the tree and moved it to another spot a few branches away. In its place, he hung Maddie's little cross-eyed cork reindeer with the uneven antlers.

"Perfect," he said. He took a few steps back and reached for Maddie's hand.

She looked over her shoulder at her mom and smiled.

28

They had only been here for thirty minutes, but already Stan could tell this wasn't a good idea.

He looked at Judith standing next to him, then up at the same sight she was looking at. At the top of the hill behind the Donnelly Center, another wildly happy child was sledding down one of the four snow runs, holding tightly to a green plastic disc. There was no way to steer these things, but that wasn't much of a problem. The runs were lined with hay bales that pretty much kept the kids heading straight downhill.

Everywhere he looked, Stan saw smiling faces and heard laughter. Except on Judith. She smiled occasionally, like when one of the children would laugh out loud. But her smile would quickly fade.

It happened again just now.

"That's Joey," Judith said. "The one that just came down the hill."

"Do we know him?" Stan asked.

"He's one of Barney and Betty's grandkids. See her son at the top of the hill? He was the one who gave the boy a push. There's her daughter-in-law, Becky, the one at the bottom of the hill who caught him. See her? Walking him around for another turn."

"Kids that age change so much from year to year, it's hard to keep up with them." He scanned the crowd. "I don't see Barney and Betty anywhere."

"They're around here somewhere," she said. "With all their kids and grandkids here, they're probably making the rounds. Might be over at those tables where the kids are making Christmas cookies."

"Do you want to go over there or stay here and watch the sledding a while longer?"

"Let's stay here . . . for a few minutes anyway."

Stan didn't figure Judith was all that interested in the sledding. It was more about not being around Barney and Betty tonight. Before they'd left to come here, Stan had asked if she wanted to hang out with them tonight and enjoy the festivities together. She'd said probably not. She didn't want to burden Betty with the job of trying to cheer her up all night. "She needs to give her undivided attention to her grandkids. That's where it belongs on a night like tonight."

Stan knew that was certainly part of the reason. But he was also pretty sure it was to avoid the pain of constantly being reminded that her kids and grandkids weren't here. She'd be glad Betty was still able to enjoy her family, but seeing them together all night would magnify her own loss.

It was Stan's loss too. He missed his kids and grandkids. But his pain seemed a fraction of what Judith was going through. The worst part of it was that she had seemed to be doing a little better this afternoon. Apparently, her ornaments class had been a great success this morning. Judith said everyone had a wonderful time, and before they'd left, one by one the children came to her saying they couldn't wait to come back next week.

Stan should've realized that bringing her to this event would set her back. The same thing had happened at the Light Up ceremony. Seeing all the parents and kids having so much fun together, and the grandparents interacting with them, stirred up memories of past years when they had been here with their family. Those memories brought pain now, not smiles. Stan wondered if that would ever change.

Would she ever get used to celebrating the holidays alone?

Twenty minutes later, they walked over to where the kids were making cookies. Well, icing cookies would be a better way to describe it. The kids spread white frosting and Christmas-colored sprinkles onto cookies that were already made. Betty and her family must've moved on to something else. Stan didn't see them anywhere.

They watched the kids for a while. Stan also watched Judith, particularly her eyes. She seemed to be enjoying this a little more.

"Hi, Miss Judith."

Stan looked toward the voice, a little girl who had just gotten in the cookie line.

"Well, hello, Maddie," Judith said. "And Taryn. And who is this?" A man was standing behind them.

"It's my dad. He came home from his trip a little while ago. Daddy, this is the teacher who helped me make the ornament."

"This is my husband, Tim," Taryn said. Tim reached out his hand.

Judith introduced them to Stan. "Have you been sledding yet?" Judith asked.

"She wants to," Taryn said. "The lines are pretty long right now, so we thought we'd come here first."

"This is our dessert," Maddie said.

"Well, they look delicious."

"Are you guys in line?" Taryn said.

"No," Stan said. "Go right ahead."

"It was nice to meet you," Tim said as Stan and Judith backed away.

"You too," Stan said.

"Oh, and by the way." Tim looked at Judith. "Taryn and Maddie absolutely loved your class. That's all Maddie talked about at dinner."

"I'm so glad," Judith said.

"Daddy said my ornament's his new favorite. He put it on the best spot on our Christmas tree."

"The best spot," Judith repeated. "That's because you did such a great job with it. Next week we'll make another one."

They said their good-byes. Judith and Stan walked away.

Stan noticed Judith was smiling again. "Maybe next year they'll add making ornaments to the roster here. Set up a few tables."

She looked up at him. "I don't see that happening."

"Why not? Making ornaments is a Christmassy thing to do. All your kids had a great time. Didn't you say there were even others gathering around in the aisles as you taught the class?"

"Yes, but it would take too long. Look at these kids. They can make those cookies ready to eat in a minute or two."

"Maybe you're right. Or maybe you could think of something a whole lot simpler. Like Anna's blue pinecone. Seems like that would go together pretty quick."

She didn't respond to that. He glanced over and saw a small line in front of another table. The night air was definitely cooling down. "Want some hot chocolate? It's right over there."

"That might be nice." She began to follow him. "But can we go home after that?"

"Sure, hon." Stan sighed and continued toward the hot chocolate table.

29

Midafternoon on Sunday, Stan was on his way to pick up Barney. He had just left Judith at the house. They had eaten lunch at her favorite barbecue place. She'd said she liked it but brought half of it home in a container. He'd hoped the sermon at church would help. At one point, the pastor had touched on the issue of people struggling with depression during the holidays. Stan wished the pastor had said more.

What he did say was for those who loved the holidays to be mindful of those who found it harder to celebrate, and to do what they could to cheer them up. And he urged those who struggled to try to keep their minds on the "reason for the season" rather than focusing on all the things that tend to bring them down during the holidays.

Stan had looked over at her at that point. He could tell by

the look on her face . . . the words did no more good than a polite pat on the head.

Taking her to her favorite barbecue place had been his feeble attempt to cheer her up. But he knew that, too, wouldn't help. He knew the reason she was so down and the only thing that would make a real difference. Judith wanted to go back in time; back to the days when their kids were still kids and all of them lived at home. Back to when the holidays were filled with their children's laughter. When the memories that now seemed to cause her so much pain were first being formed.

But those days were gone. They couldn't get them back. There was nothing Stan could do. It was an impossible situation.

Judith wasn't doing well. That dark cloud of gloom and depression surrounded her. No wonder Stan wanted to get out of the house. Even she didn't want to be there with herself.

Not when she was like this.

She was growing tired of this . . . this constant unhappiness. She had to do something, find some way to break free. She tried praying, many times. But even her prayers came off sounding like complaints to the Almighty.

A thought popped into her head from her recent conversation with Suzanne. A reminder to check her email. That's right, Suzanne said she was going to send her a link to a magazine article about empty nesters at Christmastime.

She got up out of her chair in the family room and walked over to her computer.

Stan and Barney were almost there.

They were visiting the man who owned their dream rig. Barney had followed up on his idea of buying the boat several days before Christmas, so they could take it out a few times before the fishing contest. They weren't buying it today, but with less than two weeks until Christmas, Barney thought they had better firm up the deal with this guy.

Stan wanted to see the boat again in person to make sure he really loved it, that it really was a "dream rig." They were putting an awful lot of money down on this thing. "How much farther?"

"Turn left at the next intersection," Barney said. "That's his street. Don't you remember?"

"I was only here one other time, and that was almost a month ago."

"That's right. I forgot. I've been back on my own several times since then."

"Did you talk with this guy? The owner?"

"No, I just wanted to see it. But I didn't get to. He wasn't lying about storing it in the garage."

As they approached the intersection, Stan flicked on the left turn signal. "Well, that's good for us."

"I know," Barney said. "But it's got me a little bit concerned about how we're going to keep it in such great shape once we buy it."

"I thought Betty had already agreed you could store it in your garage." Between them, Barney was the only one with a two-car garage.

"She did, and she's still fine with it. The problem is, one

of my kids has most of one side filled with their stuff. They know they need to get it out of there before Christmas. I called them last night and told them we need it out of there three or four days sooner."

The houses on this street were looking familiar to Stan. "What's the street number?"

"Forty-two twenty-two," Barney said. "It's right up here on the right." He pointed through the windshield. "Don't need to worry about reading numbers on mailboxes anyway, because there she is. I asked him if he could move it out to the driveway."

"I see it." The house had a circular driveway in the front yard that fed into a double driveway between the garage and the street. The boat was parked there. Stan pulled into the circular driveway.

"I'll go ring the doorbell." Barney hopped out of the car.

Stan got out and walked toward the boat. Any fears he had about the boat being inadequate instantly fell away. It looked beautiful, better than he remembered. Definitely a dream rig. He heard Barney talking by the front door. A moment later, he and the owner were walking in Stan's direction.

Barney spoke first. "Stan, you remember Ralph Houston."

"Sure I do." Stan stuck out his hand. He remembered the face, anyway.

Barney walked up and put both arms on the lip of the boat. "My, my. She's even nicer than I remembered."

"Barney here tells me you fellows would like to buy the boat next week and not wait until Christmas."

"If that's okay," Stan said. "He tell you why?"

"Yeah. You want to take it out a few times before that big fishing tournament. Makes sense to me."

Barney walked around to the back and looked over the outboard motor. Stan eyed the electric trolling motor at the front. It was way nicer than the one they currently owned. It had a fish-finder built right into it. He hadn't noticed that before. They might not need that dream trolling motor after all.

Stan looked up at Ralph. The man wisely stood there letting Stan and Barney fall in love with this thing all over again. He didn't need to sell it. The boat sold itself. Stan reached over and gently pushed the front pedestal seat. It swiveled around without making a sound. The gray indoor/outdoor carpeting looked brand-new. Maybe it was. He looked down at the boat trailer—not a spot of rust. Even the trailer's spare tire looked new.

Barney completed his circuit of the boat. When he came back around and stood next to Stan, Ralph asked, "So, what do you think, guys?"

"I still love it," Barney said.

"Me too," Stan said.

"Then it's settled. You guys can come pick it up next week. I'm assuming you'll have the rest of the money then, in cash."

"We will," Barney said. "I have my half together now."

"You guys want to do this today?" Ralph asked.

"Wish I could, but I can't," Stan said. "I'm almost there, but I budgeted for Christmas. So, I'm going to need one more paycheck to clear."

"That's okay. Just call me and let me know what day you're ready, and we'll make it happen."

They shook hands again and said good-bye. Barney and Stan headed back to the car. Once inside, Barney said, "Tell me that's not the most amazing bass boat you've ever seen."

"Oh, it is," Stan said. "It most definitely is."

30

Stan had just dropped Barney off at his place and was headed back home. They were already discussing their first fishing trip in the new boat. It was hard to believe, but buying the boat a few days early would make it theirs early next week. All bought and paid for. They both had Tuesday off, so that would be their first morning out on the water.

Barney wanted to get a second trip under their belt before Christmas. They discussed Friday as "Day Two." Of course, that depended on both men getting the day off, or at least the morning. Shouldn't be too hard. That would be the Friday before Christmas. Stan could offer to switch shifts with someone scheduled for the weekend. He didn't think Judith would mind, since they had no big plans for Christmas weekend this year.

That thought gave him pause as he turned onto his street.

She might say she didn't mind, but he knew better. It wasn't that she wouldn't want him to have fun or enjoy himself. It was the emotional situation she was in. Was it right for him to be off having so much fun with Barney and their new boat if that meant leaving her all alone at home? He needed to make up for it somehow, find some way to balance things out.

But was that even possible? Nothing he'd tried so far had made any difference. He pulled into the driveway and turned off the car. He didn't have to worry about looking too excited about his new boat deal. Thinking about Judith and the state she was in had wiped the smile right off his face.

He walked through the side entrance into the kitchen. "I'm home." No reply. He didn't hear any Christmas music. The thing was, he had turned the radio on to a station playing Christmas music before he'd left for Barney's. Stepping away from the kitchen into the dining room gave him a full view of the living area. He was glad to find she had at least left the Christmas tree lights on. He was about to yell out again but wondered if she might be taking a nap.

Walking toward their bedroom, he looked to his left through the open doorway into the family room. There was Judith sitting in her favorite chair, staring out the window. At least he thought she was. He stepped inside, but she didn't look up. That's when he noticed her eyes were closed. The book she had been reading had fallen to her lap. He came closer and sat on the edge of the opposite chair, which also faced the window. It made a slight noise and woke her up.

"Oh, Stan. You're home. I must've dozed off."

"You're allowed to do that. It's a Sunday afternoon."

"How'd your meeting go? Did you get to see your boat?"

"We did. I don't know if I mentioned it, but we've been

thinking maybe we should buy it a few days before Christmas." He explained why.

"That makes sense to me," she said. "Was he open to the idea, the owner?"

"He was. We're going by there next Monday after work to buy it. We have the next day off, so we'll take her out Tuesday morning. If that's okay with you?"

"With me? I don't have a problem with it." She turned her gaze back to the view outside the window.

He didn't figure she'd mind. But he minded. He minded the dead look in her eyes, the missing smile on her face. The fact that she was sitting here staring out the window again. They'd been married long enough, and he'd gotten in trouble for it often enough, for him to know you can't lecture a woman out of a place like this. But it also didn't seem like anything he did was making any difference either.

He had hoped teaching that ornaments class would have done the trick. It certainly had done *some* good . . . for a whole afternoon. But now she seemed right back to where she'd been before.

"Before I dozed off, I was thinking about doing something."

"You were?"

"But I'd need your help with it."

"With what?"

"It would involve you doing me a favor," Judith said.

"I'm up for that. What is it?"

"Could you go back up in the attic and bring down that box you call the ugly ornaments?"

This was a promising development. "Sure. You want me to do it right now?"

"You don't have to do it right now. Just some time in the—"

"No, I don't mind. I'm not doing anything just yet. I'll be right back." He left the room and headed through the kitchen out to the garage. Maybe she was finally turning a corner. She was actually going to put the ugly ornaments on the tree. He would offer to help her. They still had some eggnog left in the fridge. He could get that out, along with the nutmeg. He'd bring it out while she sorted through the box of ornaments. Get some Christmas music playing.

Reaching up, he grabbed a little wooden knob, pulled on the rope handle, and lowered the attic door steps. It didn't take long to find the box of ornaments and bring it down. It was the last thing he'd stuck up there, and he'd left it right by the edge. He walked back into the kitchen and set it down on the dining room table. Should he get the eggnog first? Maybe not. He carried the box out to the living room and set it on the coffee table. He walked over to the radio and flipped the on switch. Burl Ives was already in the middle of singing "Have a Holly Jolly Christmas."

Now, he'd get the eggnog.

"What are you doing?" Judith called out from the family room.

"Just getting things set up."

"Set up? What do you mean?"

"To hang up the ornaments, the ones the kids made."

"Hang them up? I don't want to hang them on the tree."

Stan stopped in his tracks. "You don't? What do you want to do with them?"

"Can you bring the box out here?"

"Out there? What do you want to do with them out there?"

"I thought you were doing me a favor. This is starting to feel like something else."

"Okay. I'll get them." He walked back to the coffee table, picked up the box, and headed into the family room. Setting it down on a little table beside her, he said as nicely as he could, "What are you going to do with them out here?"

She sat up and opened the lid. "I was talking with Suzanne a few days ago, and she mentioned something about wanting to have a few of the ones she made as a child. She wanted to ask me back when she moved, but she chickened out. She felt like I'd never want to part with them. The way things are now, it seemed silly not to let her have any since they're just sitting up there in the attic. I told her I'd be happy to send her some. She told me she'd think it over. Well, she hasn't called me back, and I just read an email from her, and she didn't mention it then either. I got to thinking—maybe she chickened out again and didn't want to ask me on account of how down I've been. So I decided . . . I'm not going to wait for her to call. I'm just going to box up her favorite one, maybe one or two others, and send them to her so she'll have them before Christmas. Then I decided I'd just go ahead and do the same thing for Anna and Brandon while I'm at it."

Stan's heart sank. This was awful. Not at all what he'd expected. "You sure this is a good idea?"

"I don't know if it's a good idea, but I don't see any harm in it."

Stan thought a minute. "Well, how about this, after you pick out the ones you want to send them, how about you and me hang the rest of them up on the tree? I have the music playing out there, and I was just about to fetch the eggnog and nutmeg."

She reached for his hand, so he gave it to her. "That's sweet of you, Stan. I'm afraid I couldn't take that right now, seeing all those ornaments hanging on the tree. Truth is, I'm half tempted to send all of them to the kids. It's going to be hard enough dealing with seeing them now. I couldn't deal with that every day between now and Christmas."

He sighed. "Well, don't do that. Don't give them all away. I know you feel poorly now, but you're not always going to feel this way. Maybe next year you'll feel better."

She let go of his hand. "I can't think of anything that would make me want to see these ornaments hanging on our tree ever again." She sighed. "I'm just becoming a burden to everyone, especially you. I know I need to try to move on with my life. Maybe doing this will help."

He stood there watching her slowly fumble through the box flaps and lift out the first few ornaments, the ones wrapped in green. The kids' favorites. He watched as a tear slipped down her cheek. She said she couldn't think of anything that would make her ever want to see these ornaments again. But suddenly, he could. An idea had popped into his head.

Maybe the craziest idea he'd ever had.

He stepped closer to the box, reached down, and gently grabbed Judith's hands. "Hon, I can see how hard this is for you. Let me take care of it. I'll make sure the kids get the ornaments."

31

Stan walked away from Judith, carrying the ornaments box.

"Where are you taking them?"

"Back to the garage. I thought I'd box them up at my workbench so you wouldn't have to see them."

"That's very thoughtful, but do you have the things you need to wrap them, like packing material? They're pretty fragile. I wouldn't want any of them to break."

"I don't have anything like that. I'll make a list of stuff I need and go to the store."

"They've got packing material in the office section of Walmart," she said. "You know which ornaments go to who?"

"Pretty sure I do." Of course, for Stan's idea to work, he only needed to send one ornament each. He decided to send them their favorite, so he definitely knew which ones to send. "Anything else?" He was still standing there holding the box.

"I don't think so. Oh wait, the addresses. You'll need those. I've written them all down, along with their phone numbers, on a sheet of paper hanging on the side of the refrigerator. They're under that magnet that looks like a glass marble."

"Gotcha." He started walking again.

"Oh, and Stan . . . thanks for doing this. I really appreciate it."

"You're welcome." He walked a few feet into the living room. "You want me to turn this Christmas music off?"

Judith seemed to think a moment. "No, you can leave it on." She smiled then picked up her book.

That was something anyway. If he could pull this off, pretty soon she'd be doing a lot more smiling. As he walked through the kitchen to get the addresses, another thought came to mind . . .

Pretty soon, someone else might hate his guts.

After Stan left for the store, Judith was actually feeling a little better. Almost upbeat. She had read that online magazine article Suzanne had recommended, and it made a lot of sense. It was written by a woman who seemed to completely understand what Judith was going through, because she had gone through it herself.

The bottom line was it was time to stop looking back and living in the past. Christmas memories were something to cherish and smile about, but cling to them too tightly and they'd turn sour, maybe even make you bitter. Trying to live in the past, wanting everything to stay the way it had always been, was a destructive illusion.

The trick was to move forward and be open to making

some new enjoyable memories that connect with the things and the people in your life right now. Judith instantly thought about Stan. He was real, and he was here. Their relationship wasn't the best right now, but then, what had she done lately to improve it?

The article talked about taking new pictures of things going on in your life, rather than constantly staring at pictures from the past. It then listed a number of great ideas empty-nest couples could do during Christmastime that might renew their friendship, maybe even their romance.

Judith decided she had to try.

Fifty minutes later, Stan was back from Walmart with all the packing material marked off his checklist. He'd only spent a few minutes down the office aisle. The bulk of his time was spent trying to pick out three Christmas cards for his kids. That aisle was a bit crowded, but the bigger challenge was finding a card that said just the right thing. For what he was planning to do, a few came close, but none of them hit the nail on the head.

He'd finally decided to get three blank cards that were just the same. Not that he was any good at coming up with clever things to write in cards. Judith was the writer in the family. He was amazed at the things she would think to say on cards. Usually, he'd just add something like "Love, Dad." And that would be that.

But he'd already been giving this some thought on the drive home. He could write the same thing to all three kids. They wouldn't see each other's cards since they lived in different states. He was only sending one ornament each, but to throw Judith off, he bought boxes big enough to ship two or three ornaments in. He'd just fill in the gaps with more bubble wrap.

Twenty minutes later, he had all three boxes ready to go. The only thing missing was the card to put inside. He got out the first one and tried to remember what he'd thought of on the car ride home. Took a few minutes, but it came back to him. He wrote as slowly and carefully as he could.

After finishing the cards, he set them in the proper boxes. Just as he was about to box them up, a nervous feeling came over him, like he was forgetting something.

That's right. He'd never done the math on this thing. He had better do that first, make sure the money added up. To do it right, he really needed to get on the computer, but that was back in the house. If he went there, Judith might ask him what he was doing. What would he say? Then he remembered his smartphone. Hardly used any of the features on it, but he knew he could access the internet from out here. It even had a calculator.

He pulled it out of his pocket and turned it on.

32

Three full days had passed since Stan shipped off the packages of ornaments to his children. None of them had called him yet saying they had gotten what he'd sent. He was getting a little nervous. He had paid extra to ship them 2nd Day Air. They should've gotten there yesterday. Judith was out shopping. He didn't have to be at work for another hour, so he went online to check the shipping status.

He pulled out the slip of paper from when he'd jotted down the confirmation numbers and set it beside the keyboard. One by one, he keyed in the information and was pleased to learn that the status for each package indicated they should be arriving today. Better late than never.

He hoped, and had even prayed, that his kids would be sufficiently moved by this surprise to do what he was asking them to do. In his earlier phone calls to them, each had said money troubles were the only obstacle to them coming home. What if that wasn't true? What if there were other obstacles besides money? What if only one of them said yes, or two? Should he still go through with this?

Then, of course, there was the situation with Barney and how to handle that. Stan had been avoiding his friend all week. Neither of them were great at leaving voice mails or returning them. And they'd never texted each other. But this delaying tactic could only work so long. Stan had thought it might be smarter to wait and call Barney after he had confirmed things with his kids. But Barney had just called Stan again an hour ago. This time he did leave a voice mail message.

Stan decided he had better listen to it. Picking up his phone, he pressed the voice mail app.

"Hey, Stan, it's Barney. Been trying to reach you for a few days. Hope everything's okay. Betty's talked with Judith since the weekend, so I know you're not sick. Call me back if you get this. No emergency. Just getting excited about our new boat. It'll be ours in a couple more days. Just wanted to chat, maybe talk a little more about our first fishing trip on Tuesday. Well, call me when you get a chance."

Stan's heart sank. He had been dreading this phone call. Now he dreaded it even more. What could he say? How could he even introduce the idea? He'd thought through a number of imaginary conversations over the last few days. All of them ended badly. Some worse than that.

But it had to be done.

Or did it? He thought about what Barney said about Judith having talked with Betty. Maybe that's what Stan should do, call Betty. Let Betty break the news to Barney herself. She would know what to say and when to say it. He figured it would still end badly, and Barney would still be sore at him for the next several months. At least.

Hopefully, though, it wouldn't end their friendship altogether. But that was a distinct possibility. He searched through his contacts until he found her number.

Betty picked up after a few rings. "Stan, is that you?"

"It's me."

"I thought maybe it was Judith using your phone for some reason. Are you calling me on purpose, or did you mean to get Barney?"

"No, I meant to call you."

"What is it, some Christmas surprise for Judith? Something you need me to do to pull it off?"

"Well, in a way, yes." How should he get into this? "But this is no ordinary surprise. And it doesn't just affect Judith. I think I'm going to need even more help from you with Barney."

"Barney? You're getting something for Barney? I thought you guys didn't exchange gifts. Barney's even been telling me not to get him anything this year. He said that boat the two of you are getting is his big gift."

This was going to be harder than he thought. "Yeah, that's kind of what I'm calling about."

"The boat?"

"Yeah. It will take me a few minutes to explain. But once I do, you'll know exactly what I mean about needing your help."

"Hmm. Now you've got my attention."

Stan heard their dog start to bark loudly in the background.

"Oh shoot, I'm sorry, Stan. Hold on."

She must have pulled the phone away from her mouth. He heard her yelling the dog's name several times, demanding him to stop barking. But he didn't. If anything, he was barking louder.

She got back on the phone. "I'm sorry, Stan. I really want to hear what you're saying, but someone's at the door. I better go answer it. Mind if I call you back?"

"No, but I have to leave for work in less than an hour."

"I'll call you back in a few minutes. It's probably just some kid selling something. I'm dying to hear what you have to say."

33

A few minutes ago, Suzanne got home from shopping. To her great amazement, the baby had conked out during the car ride. She had just put her down for a nap. While unloading the groceries from the car, she was surprised to see her cell phone lying on the kitchen counter. She couldn't believe she had left it home.

After picking it up, then waking it up, she checked for missed calls and texts. There was just one, a text from her sister Anna.

> Did you get a package from Dad in the last day or two? I just did, and it completely blew me away. I think he sent one to all three of us. Call me if you did and let me know your thoughts. It's pretty crazy.

Suzanne hadn't gotten any packages. But then, she had come through the garage like she always did. She hurried to the front door and opened it. Sure enough, there sat a medium-sized box addressed to her. She picked it up; it was light as a feather. As she walked it into the living room, she saw that it was from her dad. What in the world? She set it on the coffee table and almost ran to the kitchen to grab a knife.

Opening it, she found a fairly small package encased in thick bubble wrap and a red envelope. Anna's text said this package was from their father, and it certainly looked like his handwriting on the box. But why had he sent this and not their mom? It was so odd. She cut the tape holding the bubble wrap together and unraveled it.

She recognized the green wrapping paper immediately. This was how her mom had wrapped her favorite handmade ornament last year after taking it off the tree. Not just hers, but Anna's and Brandon's too. Suzanne and her mom had just been talking about these ornaments on the phone last week. Her mom had told her to think about which ones she wanted, besides her favorite, and she'd ship them to her before Christmas.

Was that what this was? But Suzanne had never called her mom back. She had decided to drop the idea, to avoid causing her mom any more sadness.

Carefully, she removed the green wrapping paper and smiled when she looked at the ornament. Jesus, Mary, and Joseph wrapped together in twine, faces like aliens from outer space. Her dad was right. It really was ugly. But she loved it, and she would love having it on her tree. She set it aside and picked up the card. She was dying to find out why her dad had sent it instead of her mom.

The first thing she noticed after opening the card was how many words had been written. At most, she was used to a line or two from him, if that. But her father's words went down both sides of the card.

She started to read:

Dear Suzanne,

Your mom said the two of you had talked recently about her sending you some of your favorite ornaments (from the ones you made as kids). You know how down she's been since Thanksgiving. Truth is, I've never seen her so unhappy. Seeing her struggle so much with this little project, I decided to take it off her hands.

I've been trying to find some way to help her out of this slump. Nothing's worked. Then I got an idea, which is why I'm sending you this ornament, and only this one.

When I called you a couple weeks back to see if there was any way you and your family could make it home for Christmas, you said you'd love to but the money just wasn't there.

Well, now it is.

I'm taking the money I've been saving for a boat and using it to bring the family home for Christmas. All of you. Spouses and kids too. If I figured it right, there's just enough to fly you all here and back, and for one family to stay at a nearby motel. (We can put up two families in the spare bedrooms. I'll let you guys work out who sleeps where.)

So, I'm sending you just this one ornament. Your favorite. And what I'm asking is for you to bring it with you on Christmas Eve—you and your family—and hang it on our tree here, back home in Mount Dora.

I know it's a lot to ask, but it would make your mom so happy. And me too.

You'll have to act pretty quick to make sure you get decent flights. You can put it on your credit cards, send me the amount, and I'll reimburse you right away. I'll even pay for the extra luggage so you can bring home any Christmas presents you bought your kids.

All my love,

Dad

P.S. I want this to be a complete surprise to your mom. Call me so we can coordinate how to make that happen.

Suzanne had a hard time reading the last paragraph and her dad's P.S. Her eyes had filled with tears.

Stan was all ready for work. It had been over ten minutes, and Betty had still not called him back. He didn't want to be a pest, but he also didn't want to have this thing hanging over him all night. He reached for his cell phone to call her, then was startled when it rang. It was Betty.

"Hey, Stan, I'm so sorry. Took longer than I thought. I'm such a sucker sometimes. I was all set to tell whoever was at the door I wasn't interested, till I saw these two middle school kids in their band uniforms. They were trying to raise money for some band trip, selling those luminaries. You know what those things are, right?"

"Luminaries? I don't think so."

"They're these white paper bags, like lunch bags. You put

sand in the bottom and candles, then you spread them out on your driveway and sidewalk. They glow real nice at night. They were just ten dollars. Anyway, guess I just added one more thing to my to-do list, unless I can get Ethan to do it for me. So, tell me what you were trying to tell me before. Something about helping you with a gift for Barney."

Stan sighed. "It's not about a gift for Barney. It's actually the opposite."

"Really?" she said. "Well, I'm listening."

Stan did his best to explain to Betty. Took him a while for all his stammering and stuttering and beating around the bush. She listened patiently, didn't say too much till he was through. And only after a lengthy pause. He wasn't sure what she'd say.

Finally, she spoke. "Why, Stanley Winters . . ." She stopped talking a moment.

Sounded to Stan like she might be crying.

"That just might be the finest thing I ever heard a man do for his wife. Feels like I'm in some kind of scene from a Hallmark Christmas movie."

Stan was so relieved. "But what about Barney? He's gonna be so disappointed. I really feel like I'm supposed to do this for Judith, like God wants me to. But it's gonna kill Barney."

A long pause. Almost too long for Stan to bear.

"That's gonna be tricky, telling this to Barney. I'm not gonna lie. That boat's all he talks about."

Another long pause.

"But I'll think of a way to break it to him. Give me a day or two. Something like this, I gotta pick just the right time."

"He'll be so disappointed, any way you say it."

"He will," Betty said. "But he'll get over it. I know he's

been worried about Judith too. We've talked about it several times."

"You have?"

"Yes. But don't focus on how Barney's gonna handle things. You're doing the right thing."

Sounded like she was choking up again.

"I want to see the look on my best friend's face when everyone shows up there on Christmas Eve next week. Be sure to record it, Stan."

"I will. But Betty, this thing isn't firmed up yet. I haven't heard back from any of my kids. I'm hoping they'll all say yes, but you never know . . ."

Suzanne reread her father's card two more times. It was still hard to believe he had done this. She'd always known he loved her mom, but he was never what you'd call the romantic type. This . . . *this* was high-end romance. Especially knowing how much Dad loved bass fishing, and how long he and Barney had been saving for that boat. She picked up her phone and called her sister.

"Hey, Suzanne," Anna said, "I'm guessing you read my text?"

"I did. Just now. I was out shopping and didn't even know the package came. After reading your text, I checked the front door and there it was."

"I'm sitting here staring at my big blue pinecone," Anna said. "When I opened the box, I almost dropped it I was so shocked. I've thought about asking Mom for it for years, ever since we moved, but never did. I just figured she'd let me have it when she was ready. Then I pulled out Dad's card and recognized his handwriting on the envelope. That was the second surprise. But then when I read what he wrote . . ."

"I know," Suzanne said. "It's just crazy. After getting your text, I had no idea what it could be. I never would've imagined this. So, are you guys gonna go?"

"We are. I haven't called Dad yet, but Bruce just called me back. He confirmed with his boss that he can get the time off. I was just about to go online and start shopping for flights. How about you?"

"I want to go. I hope we can. I've got to call Todd. I already know he's got the time off. His office is all but shutting down between Christmas and New Year's. I can't imagine him saying no."

"I wonder if Brandon can do it," Anna said. "That would be amazing if all three of us could make it."

"Did you text him yet?"

"I did, but I haven't heard back from him. He's probably still at work."

"And he's two hours back in time from you, one hour from me." Suzanne looked at her watch. "He should be getting ready to go on his lunch break in a few minutes. Maybe you'll hear from him then."

"Hope so," Anna said. "Well, guess I better check on those flights so I can call Dad."

"Are you going to book them already? My note from Dad said to call him first, so we could coordinate when to arrive."

"You're right," Anna said. "Mine did too. I was just thinking if we fly into Orlando, we could probably get there by noon or early afternoon the day before Christmas Eve. That way, if anything went wrong with the flights, we wouldn't wind up arriving too late for Christmas. I thought I'd suggest to Dad that we all rendezvous there at the house at dinnertime Christmas Eve."

"That sounds like a good idea," Suzanne said. "It's pretty easy to book flights from Dallas-Fort Worth to Orlando. I'm not so sure about Brandon, though, being out in Denver. It's not just farther away, they'll lose two hours during the trip. Maybe we should let them be the ones to stay in the motel. They could fly in the day before us."

"Good idea," Anna said. "Why don't you call him and suggest that? Dad said he was leaving the details up to us."

"All right, I'll call Brandon. Soon as I confirm things with Todd that we can definitely go."

"This is going to be so much fun," Anna said. "I can't wait to see the look on Mom's face."

Stan couldn't believe he'd already been at work for two hours. That was one nice thing about waiting on so many customers; the time flew by. It was already time for his ten-minute break. He took off his orange apron and nodded to several co-workers on his way out the front door. Before clearing the shaded area near the entrance, he pulled out his cell phone to see if any of the kids had tried to reach him.

He was happy to find two texts from the girls and a voice mail from Brandon. Walking off to the side of the store, away from the entrance, he read the texts first, starting with Anna.

Dad, Bruce and I are blown away by your generous offer to pay our way home for Christmas. Our answer is yes! Already looked into flights. We can get a flight that arrives in Orlando by 1:00 p.m. the day before Christmas Eve. Maybe we could all plan to rendezvous the following day at the house for dinner. Talked with Suzanne, haven't heard from Brandon. She thinks they can go but is waiting to hear back from Todd. Call me tonight to talk over the details. Home all night. Love, Anna

Stan smiled. One down, two to go. And from what Anna just said, it sounded like Suzanne's text might confirm they were coming too. He clicked on hers next.

Dad, this is TOTALLY CRAZY!!! Your card made me cry! First, that you'd do something like this for Mom, then make it possible for all of us to come home for Christmas. Just heard back from Todd. He said yes, definitely we'll come. Talked with Anna. They are too. We both thought Brandon's family should get the motel room, since they're coming from farther away. Call me tonight, and I'll give you the flight info. This is going to be SO EXCITING!!!

Stan said a brief prayer of thanks as he clicked out of the Messaging app and clicked on Brandon's voice mail. *"Dad, got the package with the ornament inside. Had to laugh. Still so funny when I think of our family tree cluttered with these ugly ornaments. Until I read your card, I thought you and Mom were just sending it to us as a keepsake. I did not expect the note you wrote inside. Dad, I can't let you do this. It's way too much money. And I know how much you want that boat, what it took for you to save for it. Call me when you get this. I can take calls at work. Okay then, well . . . love you."*

The message ended. Stan looked at the time. He still had a few minutes left before his break was over. He tapped

Brandon's phone number on the screen and listened as it rang. He got Brandon's voice mail and left the following message:

"Hey, Brandon, it's Dad. Heard your message. Don't worry about the money. God'll give Barney and me another boat. I really want to do this for your mom. It won't do any good now if you say no. Your sisters have already said they'll come. So most of the boat money's already gone. Please say yes. It'll make your mom so happy having us all together. And me too. Look up the flights and text me the info. But you better do it quick. Christmas is just over a week away. Your sisters were thinking your family should have the motel room. They've worked out some plan about you guys flying in the day before Christmas Eve. Call one of them to work it out. Maybe Suzanne. Your mom's going to go nuts when she sees you all. Please say you'll come. And remember, I want this to be a surprise. Well, gotta go back to work. Love you."

35

Two days later, on Saturday morning, Stan and Judith were finishing up their coffee in the family room. Stan thought about the plan; it was all set. Judith had no idea what was coming. Stan had received confirming phone calls from all three of his kids. Anna's and Suzanne's families would arrive the day before Christmas Eve in the early afternoon, then make the forty-five-mile trip north to Mount Dora. Brandon would arrive last with his family the evening before Christmas Eve, then drive here and check into a nearby motel.

Betty had said the girls' families could stay at her place until it was time for all three of them to meet at Stan's house. Betty had also agreed to let Anna and Suzanne ship their family Christmas presents to her house ahead of time. The girls said they had already bought most of the presents and were concerned they might get damaged by baggage handlers. Brandon had said his kids had asked for smaller things and he'd feel better bringing them in his carry-on luggage.

So far, Stan hadn't talked with Barney yet. Betty told him her conversation with Barney had gone as well as could be expected. He was pretty upset at first, but she knew he would start to come around after the shock of the disappointment wore off. She had called Stan last night to say he was already doing a bit better. She thought he'd be almost as good as new in a few days. She'd also mentioned some new idea they had talked over that had given Barney some hope. Stan was interested to hear more, but she wasn't ready to discuss it yet. She thought Barney might be in a few days if this new idea panned out.

Stan had another idea he hoped would pan out. His girls had given him the assignment to arrange Christmas Eve dinner and to come up with enough food for the whole family . . . without tipping off Judith. He certainly couldn't make the food; she'd be expecting a meal for two. But he hoped to have the problem solved today, maybe this morning. He needed to nail down a restaurant or catering service that wasn't already too busy *and* wasn't too expensive. He'd start making calls as soon as Judith left for her ornaments class.

"You're being awfully quiet over there."

Stan looked up at Judith. "Just thinking."

"What about?"

He should've figured that question would come next. "Uh . . . about your Christmas present."

"My present? I haven't even told you anything I want."

"I know," he said. "But I've been paying attention."

"You better not have spent too much money. We agreed on a fifty-dollar limit."

Stan had to smile.

Judith stood. "Well, I better get going. My ornaments class starts in twenty-five minutes."

The ornaments class was wrapping up. It seemed to go even better than last week. Judith was definitely feeling more comfortable in the instructor role. It was especially gratifying to see how happy the moms and daughters were and to listen to the kind words they'd said when she finished. Most of them had already gotten up from the table and said their Merry Christmases and good-byes; and to Doris's delight, instead of leaving the store, they now appeared to be shopping in the make-it-yourself area.

Judith started to clean up the worktable.

Doris came closer. "You don't have to do that. We'll take care of it."

"I don't mind."

"I know, but you've already done enough. Besides, looks like someone else wants to talk to you."

Judith looked up. Taryn and her daughter, Maddie, were coming her way. Maddie was holding up her new creation, a snowman made out of three plush pom-poms of different sizes.

"Look, Miss Judith," she said. "See?"

"I do see. You did a great job with that, Maddie."

"And you did a great job with this class," Taryn said. "We had the best time. I just wish it was longer."

"It did go by fast," Judith said. "But, you know, you can

keep this going if you want to. Make something of a tradition out of it. That's what I did. I made ornaments with
my kids every year when they were growing up. We've got
a whole box full of them at home. Of course, my kids are
grown now. But we made some fun memories every year."

"Well, this sure has been a fun memory, hasn't it, Maddie?"

Maddie nodded her head up and down. "I definitely want
to do this again."

"I'm so glad you liked it," Judith said.

Taryn leaned forward a little. "Would you mind if she
gives you a hug good-bye?"

"Not at all. I miss getting kid-hugs from my grandkids."

Maddie instantly wrapped her arms around Judith and
squeezed.

"Well, I guess we better be going," Taryn said. "Thanks
again." She took a few steps down the aisle and turned. "Will
you be teaching any more craft classes here?"

"I don't know," Judith said. "We haven't talked about
anything like that."

"She might be," Doris added.

"If you do, count us in." She and Maddie waved once
more and headed toward the front door.

"What do you think?" Doris said. "You're a natural at
this. The kids loved you. The moms loved you. And we've
sold more make-it-yourself stuff the last two weeks than we
have all year."

This was encouraging to hear. Judith hadn't said anything to Stan yet, but she had actually been thinking that
if this second class went well, she might look into what it
took to become an elementary substitute teacher. There
wouldn't be any time conflict with what Doris was talking

about, because being a substitute would happen Monday through Friday.

"I would definitely be willing to pay you something," Doris said. "We could meet and talk about some Valentine's Day crafts after the holidays. What do you think?"

"I might be interested in something like that. Can I have a little time to think about it?"

"Sure. But I'm hoping you'll say yes."

"Thanks, Doris. I probably will. I'll get back with you between Christmas and New Year's. Will you be open then?"

"Most days. We're closing early on Christmas Eve and New Year's Eve and closed completely on the actual holidays. You know how to reach me. If you want, you can just wait and give me your decision when the holidays are over."

Judith reached for her purse and bag of supplies. They hugged, said Merry Christmas and good-bye. Judith walked slowly through the store and out the front door. By the time she reached her car, she realized she was smiling. Over the last several mornings after reading her devotional, she had prayed for God to lift her out of this holiday depression and help her to stop feeling so sorry for herself. She knew self-pity was at the root of her unhappiness.

And look at how many things had improved already. The class went better than she expected, everyone who attended went out of their way to thank her, Doris wanted to hire her to teach more classes, and now she was seriously thinking about becoming a substitute teacher.

She turned on the car and remembered one more thing. *Stan.* Stan had actually thought of something to get her for Christmas this year, all on his own, without even asking her for ideas. And after reading that article Suzanne sent, she had a few ideas of her own brewing, things she and Stan could do to fill the time on Christmas Eve and Christmas Day.

36

The Day Before Christmas Eve.

Suzanne couldn't believe it. This was horrible. Their plans were ruined.

She picked up the phone to tell her sister the bad news. She couldn't imagine calling her father next. But she'd have to. The news would break his heart.

"Hello? Suzanne, is that you?"

Hearing Anna's voice brought her to tears. "Yes, it is."

"I can't really talk," Anna said. "We're actually walking toward our gate right now. Our flight leaves in thirty minutes. The airport's crazy. So many—"

"Anna, we can't go."

"What? Did you say you can't go? You mean, on the trip?"

"Yes." She tried to regain her composure.

"Why? I thought things were all set."

"They were. But this crazy cold front moved in last night. The temperature dropped way lower than they expected. All the roads and runways are covered with ice. We called the airport to check. Most of the flights are canceled, including ours. Todd's boss said sometimes these ice storms mess things up for days."

"Oh no," Anna said. "That's just awful. I'm so sorry, Suzanne. I wonder if it's going to affect Brandon."

"I don't think so. The weatherman said it's mostly affecting Texas and Oklahoma. I can't even believe it. We were all packed and ready to go."

No one said anything for a moment.

"It's not going to be the same without you guys," Anna said. "I'm going to pray for a miracle. Ice melts, right? If the sun starts warming things up and the ice melts, maybe you guys can still get out tomorrow. It will be Christmas Eve and kind of crazy, but it could still work."

"Maybe," Suzanne said. At the moment, she didn't feel all that hopeful. She was already thinking of how she would break the news to her dad.

37

The afternoon of Christmas Eve, Judith waited for Stan to come home from work. They had only scheduled his usual four-hour shift today. Since he didn't have to go in until 9:30 a.m., she'd made them a big breakfast: a sausage-and-cheese omelet, home fries, and rye toast. That was one of the ideas she'd read in that article for empty nesters. Her first "new tradition" for just the two of them . . . make a big country breakfast Christmas Eve morning.

When Stan arrived home, they would try out the second new tradition: going to see a holiday movie. She had read that movie producers always came out with big holiday releases around Christmastime. In the past, they had never paid any attention to them because their holidays were filled with family time. Now that it was just the two of them, she thought they should give it a try. Stan had always been more into movies than she was, but she had picked out one that was supposed to be a romantic comedy, and he had agreed to go.

At the very least, it would help the day go by faster. Time had slowed to a crawl the four hours Stan had been at work. She had tried calling Suzanne and Anna but just got their voice mails. She'd even sent them both a text. No reply to those either. But that shouldn't surprise her. It was Christmas Eve. Her daughters probably had their hands full trying to make the day special for their families.

Thinking she heard a car pull in the driveway, Judith peeked out the window. She was right. It was Stan. She realized right then that she had actually missed him. In part, she knew it was the change in her attitude; but it was also the way he had been treating her lately. He'd been much more attentive and thoughtful, which surprised her.

The Sunday before last, when he had come back from checking out their new boat, Stan had said something about picking it up early. This week, in fact. She wasn't sure what happened; Stan hadn't talked about it. And he and Barney never did go fishing.

She wasn't complaining. Whatever the reason, it was nice having him around and having him be so . . . what was it . . . *connected*. It reminded her of how he used to be in the years before the kids came.

The car turned off. She unplugged the Christmas tree lights and took one last look at the fairly big present Stan had put under the tree last night. Her present. She had absolutely no idea what was inside. Grabbing her purse and jacket, she headed for the door.

※

Stan got out of the car. This was getting so hard.

He had been sitting on this surprise for over a week now. He'd thought about telling Judith at least a dozen times. Every time she became discouraged or sad. Once he'd found her sitting in that same chair in the family room, staring out the window. As he walked up, she'd wiped a tear from her eye. He'd wanted so badly to tell her then.

But he'd decided to make it a surprise, and the girls made him promise he wouldn't give in. So he didn't, wouldn't. Then yesterday he got the bad news from Suzanne about the ice storm hitting Texas. He didn't know which of them took the news harder, her or him. He did his best not to make her feel bad. Wasn't anything she could do about it. But the impact of the surprise would hardly be the same this evening, without her and Todd and Brianna.

He had just spoken with Anna on the phone. Her family had landed safely at the airport yesterday afternoon. They'd driven to Mount Dora and spent the night at Betty's place. Brandon had texted him last night saying they'd arrived safely and had just checked into the motel. Last night was trash night, so Stan had stayed a little longer at the end of the driveway and called them both. It was so good to hear their voices, knowing they were so close.

Poor Suzanne.

Stan had been tempted to drop in and see Anna's and Brandon's families on his way home from work, but he couldn't squeeze it in before the time he and Judith were supposed to leave for the movie. He heard the kitchen door open and looked up. It was Judith walking this way, putting on her jacket. Her expression seemed a little upbeat. They hugged, and he opened the car door for her. She gave him a peck on the cheek as she got in. He came around the other side and got in beside her.

As soon as he turned on the car, she said, "Can you turn the heat up? I had no idea it was this chilly out."

"The temperature is supposed to drop today. A cold front's moving in. It'll probably be even colder by the time we get out of the movie."

"Well," she said, "I guess that'll be nice. Makes it feel more like Christmas."

Stan smiled. "Supposed to be pretty chilly the next few days." He started backing out of the driveway.

"You think I should go back in the house and get my coat? Will this jacket be enough?"

"I think so. The car will heat up in a couple of minutes. We'll be inside for the movie. I'm sure they'll have the heat on."

"What about after? You told me not to take anything out for dinner. Are you taking me out? Are you going to start your own new Christmas Eve tradition?"

Stan just smiled.

"What?" she asked. "Is that it? Are we going out for dinner after the movie?"

"You'll find out."

"Can't you just tell me?"

"I can't. But I promise . . . you're going to like what I've got in mind for our Christmas Eve dinner."

38

S tan had to get control of his nerves or he'd blow the
surprise. Anna and Brandon had just texted him—they
were on their way over . . . right now.

Fueling his tension was the fact that he had to keep his
phone volume turned off over the last hour. Hardly anyone
ever called or texted him, but if Judith heard his cell phone
ring several times in an hour, she would certainly start asking questions.

Another challenging moment came when they got home
from the movie. Judith said she'd enjoyed it but then said
that now that they were home and not going out again, she
wanted to change into "more comfortable clothes." Stan
knew what that meant. She'd put on her sweatpants, comfy
socks, and a soft, baggy T-shirt she liked to wear. He also
knew that wasn't an outfit she'd want to be seen in when her
kids and grandkids came walking through the door.

Fortunately, after Stan said he wished there was something they could do after dinner to take advantage of the beautiful night air, Judith suddenly remembered another one of her new Christmastime tradition ideas. Something about grabbing a cup of hot chocolate and driving through neighborhoods with the best Christmas light displays. Stan immediately agreed, then suggested she might want to hold off changing into her comfortable clothes.

Right now, Stan stood waiting for her in the living room. She had gone into the bedroom to get her book from the nightstand. He had suggested she relax in the family room a few minutes while he put together his Christmas Eve dinner surprise. But the real reason was the family room was located on the opposite end of the house from the kitchen door, where the kids and grandkids would shortly be entering.

She walked out from the bedroom hallway. "Okay, I've got my book. But you've really got me curious now about this Christmas Eve dinner. I'm actually feeling a little hungry."

Stan guided her to her chair in the family room. "If things go according to plan, I should be back to get you in about ten minutes."

"Ten minutes? What can you make in ten minutes?"

"If I told you, it wouldn't be a surprise."

"You must have called a caterer. Is that what you did? Because you better not be planning on tossing something in the microwave."

"You just start reading your book and let me worry about the dinner." The truth was, he had set things up with a caterer to arrive about forty minutes from now, giving them plenty of time together once he had sprung the surprise. He walked through the doorway leading back into the living room. "I'll just turn on some Christmas music to help set the mood."

"Not too loud," Judith said.

"I'll keep it nice and quiet." He looked at the line of sight from the family room doorway to the kitchen. This should work out fine. The plan was to have everyone gather in the driveway near the side door. Then when they were ready, he'd move Judith out to her living room chair next to the Christmas tree and make her close her eyes. Then he'd let everyone in through the kitchen. From there they could spring the surprise as they poured through the dining room into the living area.

He hurried to the kitchen and opened the side door as quietly as he could. It was already dark outside. He heard car doors open and shut out by the street. He all but ran down the driveway. His next-door neighbor had left town for a few weeks. Stan had asked Anna and Brandon to park in front of their house. As he reached the end of his driveway, the sight before him thrilled his heart.

Anna and Brandon and their spouses and children were coming toward him as a group. He couldn't help himself. He started crying. Any lingering concerns about cashing in his boat money were completely gone.

Just then, headlights appeared down the road. He was about to tell everyone to get out of the street when the car slowed, then stopped. They got out of the street anyway when they saw the car. The passenger side door opened.

What Stan saw next almost stopped his heart. It was Suzanne.

She stepped out into the street. Seeing her sister, Anna almost screamed with delight. Her husband had to cover her mouth. They all ran to greet her and Todd, who was helping the baby out of the backseat.

"What in the world?" Anna said in something of a whisper-yell. "How did you get here?"

They embraced and both started crying. Brandon's wife too.

"Todd found out the ice storm didn't reach all the way south. So he decided we could throw our things in the car and drive around it."

"You drove here?"

"Straight through," Todd said. "Seventeen hours."

Seeing all this, Stan couldn't keep it together. He walked toward Suzanne and Anna and opened his arms to a flood of hugs and kisses. He could only let this go on a few moments. "We've got to stop this. Your mom's waiting inside." He led everyone to the driveway, wiping the tears off his face. "Mom has no idea you all are here. She's sitting in the family room with a book thinking I'm getting dinner ready. We're all going to stand by the side kitchen door. But you have to be totally quiet. Okay, kids?" His grandkids all nodded. "I'll go in and bring her into the living room. After she closes her eyes, I'll come get you."

"We brought these," Suzanne whispered, holding up the Christmas ornament he'd sent. Brandon held his up too. "We thought this might be a good way to, sort of, headline the surprise."

"I remembered too," Anna said and held hers up.

"That's great," Stan said. Judith would absolutely love it. "Okay, let's go."

Just then, another car came up the street from the other direction and slowed as it reached them. When it stopped,

Stan recognized Betty in the driver's seat. She rolled down the window, a card in her hand.

"Hey, Stan."

"Hi, Betty, what are you doing here? We're about to go in and surprise Judith. Wanna watch?"

"No, I don't want to spoil it. But you're going to get it on video, right?"

"Planning to."

"I just came to drop this off. It's a Christmas card from Barney. Well, from both of us. Just hold on to it and read it after the dust settles. I think you'll like what he wrote."

Stan took the card.

"Well, I better let you all get on with your big surprise. Can't wait to hear how it goes. Merry Christmas."

Stan said Merry Christmas back and so did his kids. She drove off. A few seconds later, they all regrouped by the side door of the house. "Let's have Brandon, Anna, and Suzanne come in first," Stan said. "Holding up their ornaments. Then everyone else come in behind them."

Some of the grandchildren began to giggle. Their moms quieted them down.

"Okay, I'm going to open the door," Stan said. "Not a sound."

39

Judith thought she heard the side kitchen door open and close. She set her book on the table. It was probably Stan letting in the caterer. She was sure that's what he had done. He'd probably ordered something fancy. Something he knew she loved but something he couldn't make. She wondered what it was.

She had to admit, the extra attention he had been sending her way lately was definitely helping her emotions. By now, she had half expected to be slipping back into the darker mood she'd felt on Thanksgiving Day and the days after. But here it was, Christmas Eve, and she wasn't doing bad at all.

She heard Stan's footsteps coming her way.

"Okay, hon," he said. "I'm all set for you."

"Dinner is served?" she asked. She stood, sniffed the air. "I'm not smelling any fancy dinner smells."

"You will soon enough. But first I have something else in mind. It's a two-part surprise. For the first part, you have to close your eyes."

"Close my eyes," she repeated.

He walked toward her. "Yep. You can do it now."

She obeyed, then felt his hand take hers.

"Right this way," he said. "I'm leading you into the living room, by your favorite chair next to the tree."

She felt the bottom of the chair with her feet.

"Go ahead and sit down. That's right."

She heard him walk away. "Where are you going? Can I open them yet?"

"Not yet. In a few seconds. Oh, I love this song on the radio. I'm going to turn it up louder."

She heard Johnny Mathis singing "Silver Bells" a little louder than she wanted. "Can I open them yet?"

"In just a minute. I'll tell you."

She waited and listened to the song. Whatever the surprise was, she hoped she wouldn't have to fake enjoying it.

Before getting the kids and grandkids, Stan set his iPad up on a shelf on the hutch and turned it on. Earlier that day, Brandon had talked him through using an app that would take video with a timer. Stan had tried it already to make sure he knew how it worked. He turned the thing on and hurried to the kitchen door.

"Okay, everyone," he whispered. "Take your places. Don't make a sound." He walked ahead of them, then stood against the far wall so he could catch everything as it happened and not be in the way.

"Can I open them yet?" Judith called out.

Stan glanced at the small crowd gathered in his dining room. His three kids holding up their ugly ornaments, smiles on their faces as they looked at their mom, who was oblivious to the moment about to unfold. He looked at his grandkids, their faces beaming with excitement and joy.

It was too much. He started to lose it. "Yes, open them." She did.

The same moment, everyone yelled, "Surprise!"

Stan would never forget the look on Judith's face.

Her eyes opened wide in disbelief, trying to take it all in. "Oh my gosh, you're all here. I can't believe it!" She stood and burst into tears.

Everyone rushed toward her. Anna, Brandon, and Suzanne reached her first, then their spouses. The grandkids were hugging everyone around the legs. This went on for several minutes until Judith made sure she had hugged everyone individually.

Stan went into the bathroom, found a box of tissues, and started passing them around. Anna took charge at that moment and redirected her mother back into her chair, got everyone else to stand in a semicircle around her and the Christmas tree.

"I don't understand. How is this possible? How can you all be here?"

All the adults looked at Stan.

"It was Dad, Mom," Anna said, tears filling her eyes again. "He made it happen."

Judith looked at Stan. "But how? We don't have any money. Not this kind of money."

Brandon spoke up. "Dad used his boat money, Mom. He bought all our plane tickets."

"Stan?" Judith said, looking straight at him. The tears came again, even more than before.

It was hard to talk, but he managed to say, "Our old boat catches bass just fine."

Judith got up and put her arms around him. They hugged, tight. "I can't believe you did this," she said. "I just can't believe it."

She finally let go. Suzanne handed them both the tissue box. Judith sat back in her chair.

Stan watched as his three children stepped forward, each holding their ugly ornament. Suzanne spoke first. "Dad put this all together last week. He mailed these to us and asked if we would be willing to bring these ornaments back home and hang them on the tree where they belonged. We all said yes."

With that, Anna, Brandon, and Suzanne found a spot and proudly hung their favorite "ugly" ornament.

"They are beautiful," Judith said. "The prettiest ones on the tree."

Stan looked at his grandkids and got an idea. "I'll be right back." He hurried through the kitchen and out the side door, then over to the garage. He had never put the box with the rest of the ugly ornaments in the attic. He picked it up, then found an empty box nearby and headed back to the living room.

He set the box of ugly ornaments on the coffee table and the empty box next to the tree. Glancing at his grandkids, he said, "Do you know what's wrong with this tree? Too many store-bought ornaments." Reaching up, he removed one and replaced it with one of the ugly ornaments. "Now, that's better."

Suzanne joined in. Soon, everyone crowded around the small tree, laughing and replacing the shiny store-bought ornaments with the homemade ones.

Stan stood out of the way. Judith looked at him and silently mouthed the words "I love you."

40

While everyone was occupied decorating the tree, Stan walked over and picked up a green envelope. Inside was the Christmas card Betty had dropped off a little while ago. He'd thought about opening it in the morning, but curiosity got the better of him.

He opened the card; a little white note fell out. He picked it up and read.

Stan,

I imagine you've had quite an exciting time over the last twenty-four hours. I didn't want this thing about the boat hanging like a dark cloud over your time with Judith and the kids, so I asked Betty to get this card to you before Christmas morning.

Consider it my Christmas present. Well, really, it's from the both of us.

I admit, I was plenty sore at you when I first found out what you did last week. But God and Betty started working on me, and I started seeing things differently a few days later. Judith was in a bad way. I know that. We've never seen her so low. I also know you did what you did because you love her and felt you had to. And I know you were probably pretty torn having to give up our dream rig and feeling like you were taking it away from me too.

Here's the thing. As I write this note, I'm looking at it right now sitting in my driveway. It's all set to go.

Turns out, that guy who owned her was pretty desperate to sell her. When I told him we had to back out, he started talking a new deal. Betty reminded me we finished up with a $3,000 bank CD last month. Barely earned a lick of interest on it. Wasn't sure what to do with the money. She suggested I offer the man $8,000 for that boat, and he jumped at it.

So our dream rig is now my dream rig. Course, I'll still let you fish with me, and I'll still need you to go in half on the gas and bait. If you're okay with that, we can take her out soon as you send those kids and grandkids back to wherever they came from.

Merry Christmas, my friend.

Barney

Judith looked up, saw Stan by the hutch reading some kind of note. Whatever it was, it seemed to be getting him upset. She saw tears in his eyes. New ones. She got up to see if everything was all right.

"I'm fine," he said. He wiped his eyes and handed her the note. "It's from Barney."

She took it and read it. As she did, he put his arm around her and squeezed tight. When she was done, she couldn't believe it. The hardest part about this amazing thing Stan had done for her was knowing how much he and Barney had wanted that boat.

And here God worked it out that they got to have their dream rig after all.

"Dad? Mom?" It was Brandon over by the Christmas tree. He must have noticed the two of them by the hutch reading this note. "Is everything okay?"

"We're fine, son," Stan said. "Actually, more than fine."

Christmas Eve came to a close a few hours later. Brandon and his family had left for their motel room. They'd be back in the morning to open up presents. Anna's and Suzanne's families were occupying the guest rooms. The two oldest grandchildren were sleeping on an air mattress in the family room, but against the far wall so they couldn't see into the living room. All the presents were wrapped anyway, so there was no chance of them finding out what they were getting by sneaking a peek.

Judith was almost finished getting ready for bed. Stan, already in his pajamas, had gone out to give the house a once-over, turn off the lights, and make sure the doors were locked. Just before he left the room, he told Judith some more good news. Anna and Brandon had told him they were so affected by the sacrifice he'd made that they had decided to put it in their budgets next year to make it home for the holidays, one for Thanksgiving and the other for Christmas.

But there was even better news coming from Suzanne. She and Todd had decided to start looking for a transfer back to Florida. He thought it might happen about ten months from now, so they'd be here, one way or another, for both holidays next year.

It was almost more blessings than she could bear.

She had finished getting ready and was just about to get into bed when she realized Stan hadn't returned. She went to check on him and found him standing in the center of the living room, staring at the Christmas tree.

Walking up, she wrapped her arms around his waist, then came around to his side.

Stan looked at her and said, "I loved hearing the kids telling their kids all the stories behind each of those handmade ornaments. You gave our kids some incredible Christmas memories. You know that?"

"I suppose," Judith said. "But I think what you did here tonight gave this family a Christmas memory none of us will ever forget. I still can't believe you did it."

He patted her shoulder. "And I can't recall a time I ever enjoyed myself more."

"I can't recall a time I've ever felt so loved."

He put his arm around her shoulder. "What a sight," he said. "Never saw so many presents under a tree."

"Or," she said, "a tree with so many fancy ornaments."

Dan Walsh is the award-winning author of *The Unfinished Gift*, *The Homecoming*, *The Deepest Waters*, *Remembering Christmas*, *The Discovery*, *The Reunion*, and the Restoration series. A member of American Christian Fiction Writers, Dan served as a pastor for twenty-five years. He lives with his family in the Daytona Beach area, where he's busy researching and writing his next novel.

Meet Dan Walsh at
www.DanWalshBooks.com

Learn more interesting facts,
read Dan's blog, and so much more.

Connect with Dan on

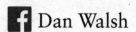 Dan Walsh

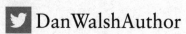 DanWalshAuthor

Heartwarming Tales of *Love* and *Loss*

"Dan Walsh is quickly becoming one of my favorite go-to storytellers for sweet romance and intricately woven parallel storylines."

—USA Today, *Happily Ever After*

With deep insight into the human heart, consummate storyteller Dan Walsh gently weaves a tale of a life spent in the shadows but meant for the light. Through tense scenes of war and tender moments of romance, *The Reunion* will make you believe that everyone can get a second chance at life and love.

Revell
a division of Baker Publishing Group
www.RevellBooks.com

Available wherever books and ebooks are sold.

In 1962, life was simple, the world made sense, and all families were happy. And when they weren't, everyone knew you were supposed to pretend.

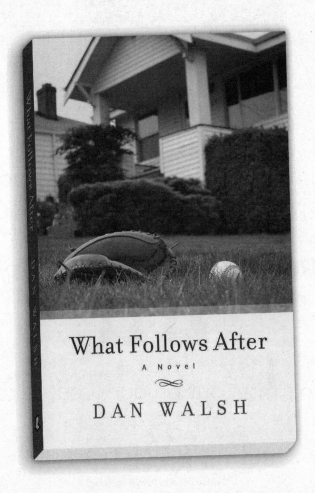

"Dan is an artist who paints with words, and his canvas is the novel, where he uses different colors and hues of words to create a masterpiece. *What Follows After* is a marvelous old-school tale illustrating the importance of faith and family. It's a story that will surely touch your heart and soul."

—**John M. Wills,** *New York Journal of Books*

Revell
a division of Baker Publishing Group
www.RevellBooks.com

Available wherever books and ebooks are sold.